*A
Harlequin
Romance*

OTHER

Harlequin Romances

by ELIZABETH HOY

THE
BLUE JACARANDA

by

ELIZABETH HOY

HARLEQUIN BOOKS

TORONTO
WINNIPEG

Harlequin edition published August 1975

SBN 373-01901-7

Original hard cover edition published in 1975
by Mills & Boon Limited.

CHAPTER I

From the fourteenth floor window of her high-rise hotel Lena Shannon looked down at the brilliantly lit city with its church spires and clustering rooftops. There was the dark sheen of a river, the curve of a brilliantly illuminated motorway bridge spanning the water. Brisbane City at night. Thirteen thousand miles from home and she wasn't yet at the end of her journey. Tomorrow there would be an eighty-mile coach ride to Windara, where Uncle Tom Shannon's estate was situated. If she decided to go there.

Drawing the curtains across the window, she turned back to the neat impersonal room and got into the single bed awaiting her. When she had put out her bedside lamp she lay staring into the darkness. There was so much to be decided before she allowed herself to fall asleep, though the need for sleep was almost overpowering. Twenty-eight hours in the air had taken their toll, the muted sound of the engines in the big jet, the strange mix-up of days and nights as the hours changed to coincide with the international time zones through which they passed. It had left her feeling a bit lightheaded and bewildered, so that the events which had immediately succeeded her arrival at Brisbane airport now seemed like a confused dream. A dream which she *must,* in the short time available, transmute into reality. She wouldn't be able to sleep until she did, she told herself, and promptly lost consciousness. The comfortable bed, the warm Queensland darkness, the distant drone of the city traffic were all too much for her weary mind and body.

When she woke with a start daylight was filtering

through a crack in the drawn curtains. Filled with alarm, she sat up and glancing at her wrist watch found it was seven o'clock. In two hours' time Mr McKindry would be calling on her, ready to hear if she had decided to accept the strange terms of her Great-Uncle Tom Shannon's will or not. That she should have time to make this decision was the object of her stop-over in the Brisbane hotel.

'If you favour your uncle's terms and wish to stay in Australia,' Mr McKindray had said yesterday, 'I will put you on the mid-morning coach for Latonga, the township nearest to your uncle's estate. I can phone Mr Rod Carron in plenty of time for him to meet you. You'll have no difficulty in knowing when you've actually reached Latonga, since it's the journey's terminal.'

Rod Carron! The name hit her now like a blow over the heart. She buried her face in her hands. 'I can't go on with this; I can't!' she whispered aloud in the lonely hotel room.

With a goaded air she jumped out of bed and flung back the curtains. There was the city spread before her, gilded with the early morning sunlight, even at this hour a hot, hard gold. The distant river was a flashing sword beneath its great curving bridge. Already the traffic-congested streets were busy with pedestrians on their way to work. At home, she thought, it would be a damp grey October morning. Or no . . . it would still be yesterday evening. Oh, those time zones . . . she couldn't work them out! 'Jet lag,' they called it. A reviving shower in the adjoining bathroom helped to clear her head and give her courage. As she dressed she reviewed the events of the past astonishing weeks. But astonishing as they had been nothing had prepared her for the sheer in-

6

credibility of the situation which awaited her here in Queensland.

It had all started the September evening she had returned from the London office where she worked to her Earl's Court bed-sitter to find Uncle Tom's letter awaiting her. He was one of the few relatives left to her since the death of her mother three years ago. Her father had died when she was very young and she did not remember him. Her mother had been everything to her, and there had been a dark interlude indeed after her death. But time inevitably does its healing work and Lena had begun to take interest again in her life in the flatlet community, a world mostly inhabited by office-working girls like herself. Lena had shared her flat with two others, so she was not without friends. And there was kindly Aunt Meg and the cousins out at Ealing, always ready to welcome her. Life was by no means lonely, enlivened at intervals by passing romantic attachments. So far there had never been anyone important enough to Lena to make it more than passing. She had been busy and contented until the bombshell of Uncle Tom's letter had crashed into her orderly little world; her father's adventurous uncle who as a young man at the end of his war service had departed for Australia to make a fortune for himself. He had written to Lena and her mother spasmodically throughout the years, sending generous money gifts at Christmas time. 'A lonely old bachelor,' he had once described himself, telling Lena she was his nearest relative and that her father had been his favourite nephew in the distant years gone by. The exigencies of his growing fruit farming business and a dislike of travel had prevented him from making the trip to England to see them during her mother's lifetime, and after that he had pleaded the burden of his increasing years.

He had mentioned this again in the letter Lena had read with growing excitement that September evening. He was nearing the end of the road, he wrote, and had an increasing desire to see the younger Tom Shannon's only daughter. Would she not arrange her affairs so that she could come and spend a few months with him? 'The beautiful property of Windara awaits you,' he had pleaded. 'Acres and acres of sugar cane fields, pineapple plantations, fields of ripening strawberries, and bush land stretching for miles along the bank of a wild, wide river. I think you would enjoy it all. Do come. All expenses paid, of course. You would be doing a great kindness to an old man.'

Lena had sat with the letter in her hand, imagining it all. A trip to the other side of the world to a place all sunshine and wild rivers and sugar cane and pineapples. It was a temptation too great to resist. 'There are horses to ride,' Uncle Tom had urged, 'a boat on the river, and we're not all that far from the lure of the various surfing beaches . . .'

After the initial shock of delighted surprise Lena had told Uncle Tom she was on her way, and set about making her preparations for the journey. It hadn't been difficult to give up her work at the office. There would be plenty of similar jobs awaiting her in a secretary-starved London on her return. So she had booked her flight well in advance, obtained a new passport, and had the necessary inoculations. All this took about three weeks. As the days went by her excitement mounted. Sometimes it seemed as if the moment of departure would never come, but at last she found herself seated beside one of the little windows in a luxurious jumbo jet. Sleeping, eating delicious meals, having brief glimpses of strange exotic

8

places while the great plane re-fuelled, the mixed up days and nights went by. And then they were touching down at Brisbane airport. Passing through various formalities of arrival, Lena came to the transit lounge where anxious friends and relatives scanned the ranks of incoming passengers. She had told Uncle Tom, who had promised to meet her, that she would be wearing a pale green summer coat and carrying a red suitcase. But peering through the crowd she could see no sign of him. There would, she had thought, be no difficulty in recognising him from the recent photograph he had sent her — a large, bluff, rather handsome old gentleman with an engaging smile. But there was no one who answered to this description in sight.

'Miss Lena Shannon?' The elderly gentleman who had accosted her was a very travesty of the uncle she had expected. Small, thin, nervous-looking, with a drooping white moustache, he gazed at her with an apologetic air.

'My name is McKindry,' he had announced, when she had confirmed her own identity. 'I'm your uncle's solicitor. He himself was unable to meet you.' His voice trailed away in an uneasy fashion. 'In fact,' he went on, 'I have some rather bad news for you, Miss Shannon. Your uncle was taken seriously ill about a fortnight ago. He didn't want you to be told this — he was anxious for you to continue with your plans as arranged.'

'But of course,' Lena burst in eagerly. 'If he's ill it's all the more reason I should be with him.'

Mr McKindry gave her a hunted glance and picked up her suitcase, which looked far too heavy for him 'I think we'd better go to the hotel where I've booked a room for you, so that you can have a meal and a rest before completing your journey,' he said.

On the drive to the hotel through some rather tatty suburbs he was uncommunicative, parrying Lena's anxious questions about her uncle's illness, saying it would be better if they did not discuss the situation until they reached the hotel. The suburbs were left behind and Mr McKindry now kept on pointing out buildings of interest in the wide and imposing central streets. But Lena scarcely listened. What ill tidings was this nervous little man concealing? It was all so tragically obvious in the end that she was hardly surprised when, sitting in the hotel lounge, fortified by the glass of sherry Mr McKindry had insisted upon, she learned that her uncle had died more than a week previously.

After a brief interval of shocked silence she asked, ' Why didn't you tell me . . . stop me taking the journey out?'

'Because,' replied Mr McKindry firmly, ' your presence at Windara is more than ever necessary. Your uncle has made considerable provision for you in his will.' He had come to a full stop then and gazed at her through the thick lenses of his spectacles in some confusion.

' It is,' he murmured thickly at last, ' in some ways rather a strange will.' Slowly and with many legal ambiguities he had disclosed its bizarre contents. Lena listened in stunned disbelief. She was to be co-inheritor to the Windara estate together with one Rod Carron, a trusted friend and companion to the old gentleman in his declining years, during which time the said Rod Carron had taken on most of the work of the property. It was Tom Shannon's wish that his niece Lena Shannon should ultimately marry Rod Carron. If that condition were to remain unfulfilled the estate was to go to a distant cousin who lived in New Zealand. But there was no hurry. Lena and the Carron man were to have six months in which to get to know one another and make up their minds. During that period they would be handsomely paid out of the estate. Carron, it emerged, was a widower with one small daughter.

'Naturally,' Mr McKindry pointed out, 'it's important for him in his circumstances to be able to look forward to at least another six months at Windara. If either of you were to refuse this six months' probation the estate would revert at once to the legatee in New Zealand.'

Lena's shocked impulse was to blurt out, 'Let it revert then . . .' But she bit back the words, trapped by a feeling of responsibility towards the unknown Carron. A needy widower whom, if she defaulted, she would be depriving of six months' livelihood. 'What is he like, this Carron?' she demanded.

Mr McKindry looked baffled, searching no doubt in his dry legal mind for the cautious phrases which would deal safely with the question.

'He's a sound chap from all accounts,' he brought out at last. 'I've always found him pleasant-mannered, unobtrusive. Not, of course, that I've had much to do with him. But your great-uncle thought very highly of him.'

'Does he live at the house at Windara?' Lena demanded, stifling the growing sense of outrage.

'I believe he always has done so during his years of working on the estate. But I gather he has moved recently to a bungalow which is part of the property. There is a housekeeper at Windara who's been with your uncle for years. She would stay on during the trial six months and run the domestic affairs as she always has done.'

'And what should I be doing?' Lena asked, feeling more and more like Alice in Wonderland.

'Getting to know the workings of the estate, I presume,' replied Mr McKindry. 'With the possibility in mind that it might become your property.'

'Shared with the Carron man,' Lena shuddered.

'Naturally you will have to give the matter a good deal of thought,' Mr McKindry conceded.

And throughout the confused hours of the previous day she had tried to do just that. But without much success. There was too much involved and her thoughts wouldn't come clearly. Partly because she was still suffering from ' jet lag ', the curious disorientation resulting from the long flight.

Now, even with the night's rest behind her, she still felt bewildered. There was the shock of Uncle Tom's death, the disappointment of not being able to see him, talk to him, having travelled across the world for that purpose. Instead she was confronted with the bizarre choice he was demanding of her. Offering her a lavish Australian property — plus an unknown husband. And if she refused this offer she would return to office work and a bed-sitter in London. The prospect seemed bleak. But the alternative remained utterly crazy.

'Give it a try,' Mr McKindry advised when later he sat with her over breakfast in the hotel dining room. 'It's what your uncle wished for you,' he emphasised. 'He had, it seems, had warning of his state of health from his doctor when he wrote and invited you to come to Australia for a visit — hoping, no doubt, that he would be able to persuade you to remain permanently. He knew he had not long to live.'

'If he'd just left me the estate with no strings attached,' Lena said.

'It wouldn't have been easy for you to run the fruit farm alone. It's a sizeable concern.'

'This Rod Carron. . . .' She hesitated over the hated name. 'Couldn't he have remained on as foreman or bailiff, or whatever you call it in Australia?'

'He had been with your uncle for about seven years,' Mr McKindry reminded her. 'And in that time had, I gather, become more like a son to the old man than an employee.'

'Then why didn't he leave the estate to him and be done with it?' Lena pursued crossly.

'Clearly it would be because of his strong family feeling. He wanted Windara to remain in the possession of Shannons and the descendants of Shannons.'

'Only if I *did* go along with his wishes the descendants would be Carrons, not Shannons,' Lena pointed out, and found herself blushing hotly at the implications.

Mr McKindry, tactfully averting his glance, said gently, 'Strange as all this must seem to you, my dear, why don't you go and have a look at Windara? There's no obligation on you to stay there for the full six months of probation if you don't feel like it. But surely there could be no harm in giving the matter a week or two?'

'All right,' Lena found herself agreeing with a sinking feeling. Before she had time to change her mind Mr McKindry was on his feet, saying he had better put a call through to Windara straight away, to let Rod Carron know she would be on the midday coach for Latonga.

'I wasn't able to speak to Carron himself,' he told Lena when he rejoined her. 'It was Mrs Clarens, the housekeeper, who answered the phone. Carron was out on the farm, it seems, but Mrs Clarens assured me that someone would be at the coach terminal to meet you.'

Committed now beyond withdrawal, Lena went up to her room to prepare for her departure. There was still a couple of hours to fill in, so when they had left her baggage at the coach station Mr McKindry took her on a conducted tour of the city. Abstractedly Lena gazed at old and new buildings, wide main streets with prosperous-looking shops and an unexpected cul-de-sac where a hundred-year-old tree-shaded stable yard had been preserved in its original rural simplicity — only the stables were now used as garages for expensive cars. At last, after a snatched early lunch of coffee and sandwiches, she took her seat in a large comfortable coach. When it started on its way, leaving Mr McKindry waving a friendly goodbye from the adjoining pavement, her heart felt cold and small in her breast. What on earth was she letting herself in for?

During the two hours which followed she gazed out of the window at her side, only vaguely aware of the rather monotonous road they travelled. At intervals there were wayside garages, the occasional homestead; but for the most part it seemed a deserted land, a patchwork of dull-coloured vegetation stretching for limitless miles to a far horizon. Until at last they were cruising down the main street of a small bright town, gay with flowering trees in the brilliant afternoon sunshine.

How was she going to recognise her contact from Windara? Lena wondered as she stepped down from the coach. All the other passengers seemed to know exactly where they were going. There was no sign of anyone answering to the description of the middle-aged Mr Carron, and soon she was left standing alone by the office door of the terminal, her suitcase on the

14

pavement beside her. Presently a young man with fair hair, burned to chestnut, and a deep tan to match approached her with an engaging air of diffidence.

'Are you by any chance Miss Shannon?' he asked.

She summed him up as she said that she was, meeting his steady glance. His eyes were grey, very direct and clear, with a whimsical light in them, his features well cut from the broad high brow to the strongly cleft chin.

'I'm from Windara,' he offered. 'Guess you're tired after your long trip. How was the flight?' he asked, as he picked up her case.

'Super,' she answered shortly, with no inclination to enter into an account of her journeying.

Her escort led the way across the street. Like most of the younger men in the little town he was dressed in white shorts and shirt, with white cotton socks pulled up over his shapely brown calves. His bare arms too were brown and aggressively muscular. There was a shiningly clean look about him, as if he had just stepped out from under a shower, his thick fair hair slicked back damply. Walking by his side, Lena wondered where was the car for which they must surely be making. 'How far is Windara?' she asked.

'A good mile or so. We go by river,' the young man replied surprisingly.

Even as he spoke they had turned down a side street and there was the great wide river before them, and a rather makeshift landing stage to which a small motor launch was moored.

'Here we are,' announced her companion. Why hadn't he introduced himself? Lena wondered, and concluded that he was one of the workers on the farm — a superior one by the look of him; some sort of an expert on sugar cane growing perhaps.

Politely he helped her to step down into the boat,

15

holding her hand in a strong cool grip. Her own hand, she was aware, was warm and moist. It was the hottest hour of the afternoon and she could feel the force of the sunshine like a palpable weight on her thinly clad shoulders. There was a covered cabin to give shelter from the sun, flanked by comfortably upholstered seats, and at the front end of it in the prow of the craft a raised platform on which was set the steering wheel and look-out window. The sides of the cabin were fitted with sliding windows, now drawn back to admit a welcome breeze as the launch drew away from the landing stage.

Swinging the craft into mid-stream, the young man steered northwards. Lena gazed about her, enchanted by the beauty of the scene. The river was so wide it was almost a lake, the distant banks covered with thick vegetation. The current was strong, flowing against them, and she could see by the partly submerged bushes on the edge of the banks that the water was in flood. Large strange-looking birds flapped lazily in the distance. 'Cranes,' the young man supplied when Lena asked what they were. 'And there's an ibis,' he added.

Lena looked at the stork-like bird with its long cruelly curved beak. 'I want to see black swans,' she said. 'In a guide book I read before I came out here it specially mentioned black swans in connection with Queensland rivers.'

'So you've been doing your homework?' The tone was cynical. 'And you've come all the way to Australia to look at black swans.' There was no mistaking the mockery now. 'Or could there have been a less aesthetic motive? But whatever it was, it was brave of you to come. I never seriously expected that you would. But I suppose the lure of the Windara property was too much for you.'

16

Lena felt the blood rush to her cheeks. Whoever he was, this young man evidently knew something about Uncle Tom's strange will. She was glad he was standing at the wheel with his back to her so that he could not see her scarlet face, or witness her confusion. But she ought not to be so surprised, she told herself. In an isolated country place like Windara the eccentricity of Uncle Tom's will, once it had leaked out, would be a subject for gossip, especially among the employees on the property. They would be wondering what she would be like; this unlikely legatee who was to take a husband as well as a fortune. But this reasonable reflection didn't blind her to the impertinence of this brash young man. She said in a tight voice, 'I came to Australia knowing nothing about the property, expecting to find my uncle alive. . . .'

'I know,' her companion broke in. 'I'm sorry. His death must have been a shock to you. But not, I guess, as big a shock as his will . . . giving you six months in which to make up your mind to marry a total stranger.'

Indignation welled up and stronger than indignation the impulse to defend herself. 'I should have been told all this before I left England. Instead of which I was allowed to fly across the world to be confronted when I arrived with a situation in which I'm to be responsible for the welfare of this man Carron . . . a middle-aged widower with a child to keep. If I refused the terms of the will asking me to give the matter a six months' trial I should, it seems, have been doing this man out of a considerable sum of money. Even without marriage coming into it at all I was trapped.' She could hear the words pouring from her even as she wondered why she should bother to explain herself to this ill-mannered stranger. Her annoyance with herself only made her all the more angry.

17

'If it's strange that I've come here,' she went on, 'it's even more strange for Mr Carron to have let me come. If he'd been half a man he could have refused the whole bizarre deal. Taking himself and his child off and forgone his six months of payment from the estate, at the expense of an unknown girl!'

The young man turned from the wheel to give her a scornful glance. 'So it's sheer altruism which brings you here! How touching. Pity for Carron is your motive. Is that what you're telling me?'

'Why should I bother to tell you anything?' she choked. 'Is it anything to do with you what my motives may or may not be? Who are you anyway?'

He hesitated a moment, then turned back to his steering. 'Just one of the people who keep Windara going,' he answered her question. 'Aren't you longing to hear about it? The fields of sugar cane, the acres of pineapple. Don't you want to know just how much money it brings in annually?' There was no mistaking the insolence now.

Lena stood up. 'How dare you talk to me like this?' Tears of rage filled her eyes and she was shaking. 'I'd be glad if you would remember our respective positions and get on with the navigating — which at the moment, may I remind you, is your sole concern!'

'Sorry, ma'am!' He touched a blond forelock. She could see from the angle of his head that he was grinning. 'I'll try to keep my humble station in mind.'

She turned from him to walk from the small covered enclosure out on to the open deck in the stern. There were slatted seats here. She could stay here for the rest of the brief journey . . . seething over the needless encounter. Why had she let it develop? It was maddening that it should have spoiled the run up this beautiful river. She mustn't make too much of it, she told herself. Perhaps all Australians were as cheeky and outspoken as this blond, self-assured young man. A country of fierce independence where Jack was as good as his master. Indeed the word 'master' was probably not in their vocabulary at all. But no amount of reasonable arguing with herself could take the sting out of the things the young man had said to her. Implying that she was a fortune-hunter . . . willing to endure any humiliation rather than forgo becoming the mistress of Windara. With an unknown husband thrown in. But that, of course, was how it would appear to the casual onlooker.

The whole thing was intolerable. Why had she agreed to come here this morning? . . . letting Mr McKindry pressure her into it, saying she could give it a couple of weeks at least. That it would be less than fair to all concerned if she refused. She no longer cared whether she was being fair or not. She would stay in Australia just long enough to arrange her flight back to England — not a moment longer! Tomorrow she would take the coach back to Brisbane and go straight to the nearest travel agent's office. . . .

The boat swerved sharply round a bend which revealed a thickly wooded island. High above the trees in the centre of the island rose an immense volcanic rock, roughly peak-shaped.

'Caloola Island,' the young man called out to her from the wheel cabin. 'Won't you come forrard and let me tell you about it? There's a local legend about it which might interest you.'

'I'm quite comfortable where I am,' Lena returned coldly.

'Oh, well,' her companion replied easily, 'I'll tell you the tale all the same. It will shorten the journey for you — and, as it happens, it's oddly relevant.

19

'Caloola,' he repeated. 'It's a girl's name. She was very beautiful. . . . But let me begin at the beginning.'

The rock in the middle of the island, he said, was supposed by the Aborigines of ancient times to be sacred. Various feasts and ceremonies were conducted in its shadow.

'Away back in the Dreamtime,' the young man continued, 'which is the Aboriginal name for the "mythological" period of their history, Caloola was brought to the island — subsequently named after her — to be betrothed against her will to Yandina, an ageing chief, but a man of great importance. Caloola was in love with a handsome young warrior named Coolum, and was heartbroken at the prospect of being forced into marriage with old Yandina.' He turned from his steering wheel to give Lena a wicked grin.

'Rings a bell, doesn't it? Arranged marriages are, it seems, nothing new in these parts!'

'You're making this up,' she accused indignantly.

'Honestly I'm not. At least there are no handsome young warriors on the horizon of our modern version.'

'There certainly are not!' Lena returned with force. Why was she allowing this ridiculous conversation to continue? Only that there was something compelling in the grey eyes fixed on her, a hint of seriousness beyond banter.

'Coolum,' continued the young man, 'turned up at the betrothal feast and engaged Yandina in mortal combat — mortal at least for poor Coolum. His wounded body was flung into the river. Caloola threw herself in after him and was drowned with him. The story goes that she can be seen here on moonlit nights, sitting on the shore of the island combing her long hair and wailing softly, mourning her lost love.'

'At which point,' said Lena, 'the bell stops ringing.

There are other ways of avoiding an unwanted marriage besides throwing oneself into a river.'

'Of course there are.'

'One can throw oneself into the comfortable seat of a jumbo jet and take off for a distant shore.'

'Quite. And I wasn't making sinister comparisons. Only at this point on the river, when we're carrying newcomers, we always tell them the story of Caloola Island. Invariably it goes down very well. But it might have been more tactful if I'd kept off it today.'

'It would certainly be more acceptable if you were not quite so talkative,' Lena returned frigidly.

'My renewed apologies,' the young man muttered, sounding as if at last his insufferable self-possession had been slightly dented. And for the remainder of the journey he kept silent. Until approaching a badly kept landing stage he announced, 'Here we are! Windara!'

Lena looked about her in bewilderment, confronted by what seemed to be an utter wilderness. There was no sign of a dwelling place, or of cane fields or plantations of pineapples. Nothing but the towering dark gum trees and the thick low-growing vegetation of typical 'bush' country. The silence was profound as they tied up. The loneliness of the place filled her with apprehension. She ignored the hand held out to help her from the launch.

'I can manage, thanks,' she said dismissively, stepping up on to the landing stage.

'The car is just down the track,' her companion announced, leading the way to an opening in the trees. It revealed a rough dirt road bordered on one side by what looked like a toy railway line that branched aside to disappear into the bush which ran parallel to the river.

As they left the river the heat became intense, the late afternoon sunshine pouring down through the opening in the trees to concentrate itself on the uncovered way. It was like walking into a furnace.

The car turned out to be a shabby station waggon. As they approached it a long line of trucks came along the little railway line. They were open trucks, all closely packed with some kind of agricultural product. Like untidy wheat sheaves, Lena thought.

'Some of our sugar cane,' her companion announced. She gazed at the winding snake of trucks, interested in spite of herself. As it drew level with them, the train stopped and two young men, naked to the waist, jumped out of the leading cabin, which obviously contained the engine power.

'Hi-ya!' they hailed the blond young man companionably.

'Hi!' he responded. 'You're getting the load off in good time, I see.' His tone held commendation.

'We aim to be at Dundoochy by teatime.'

'Good-oh,' responded the blond young man. Then turning to Lena: 'Meet Miss Shannon!'

'Hi-ya, miss,' the train drivers responded in chorus, nodding to her familiarly. More easy-going Australian manners, Lena thought. There was no sign of employee diffidence in their greeting. The independent Aussies. But she liked the look of them. They all had the same frank open faces as her escort, the same burnt blond hair and deeply tanned skin. She felt the curiosity in their intent glances and wondered how much they knew of the circumstances which had brought her here. Probably every bit as much as the man who had elected to meet her coach at Latonga.

'By the way, Rod,' one of the train drivers was saying, 'there's a message waiting for you in the office.

There's been a bit of a hold-up with that fertiliser you were expecting. It won't arrive now until the end of the week.'

Rod! Lena turned a startled look at the young man by her side.

'Thanks, Ed,' he was saying carelessly, obviously unconcerned about the delayed fertiliser. 'Well, we'd better be getting along. Miss Shannon will be tired after her journey.' He put a hand familiarly beneath Lena's elbow, ushering her towards the waiting car.

'So long, then!' The train drivers with an affable nod returned to their sugar cane waggons.

When they reached the car Lena shrugged off her companion's hand and turned to him enquiringly. 'Rod?' she said. Perhaps it was a common name in these parts.

But the blond young man was nodding, and grinning wickedly. 'Rod Carron at your service, ma'am!' The mock humility was the last straw. Lena's face flamed, and with it her temper.

'Of all the mean, low-down tricks!' she stormed. 'Passing yourself off as an employee on the estate, trying to worm out of me what I felt about my strange involvement with Windara in general and yourself in particular!'

Still with that insufferable grin on his face he opened the car door for her. But she made no attempt to get in. In fact she doubted if she ever would. Her impulse was to turn round and demand to be taken back to Latonga in the motor launch. And from there she would board the first coach heading for Brisbane and the airport.

CHAPTER II

Rod Carron's reaction to her outburst was to laugh aloud. 'That's not quite how it was,' he corrected her. 'I didn't start off with the intention of passing myself off as a worker on the farm. But when you so obviously concluded that I was and launched into a tirade against the hated Rod Carron, I couldn't resist the impulse to let you go on. And from then on the situation more or less ran away with itself. I was particularly intrigued to hear myself described as a middle-aged widower. I'm just twenty-seven. I lost my wife seven years ago when our little girl was born.' There was no laughter in his voice any more. His eyes held a haunted look for a moment.

Then he said gently, 'I'm very sorry. But honestly, once you'd declared your scorn for the man who had allowed you to come here under the terms of the late Mr Shannon's will I knew the truth of my identity would be embarrassing. I just funked telling you. I thought vaguely that I would break it to you gently before we reached the house. Then the lads came along with the sugar load. . . .'

'It's all very well your trying to wriggle out of it,' Lena accused. 'It was you yourself who started the invidious remarks, mocking me about the black swans, saying I'd come out to Queensland solely to find them. Then telling me I was foolhardy to have risked the trip. Implying that if I'd been nicely brought up I would never have contemplated it . . . only you supposed that I was interested in getting my hands on the Windara property. . . .'

'Okay, okay, you've made your point. I've behaved

like a heel.' Ill temper flashed in his glance. 'But we're both "trapped", as you put it, in this crazy situation. So let's make the best of it, for the moment.'

'A moment is too long. I can't get back to Brisbane quickly enough. . . .'

'You'd better come up to the house and get a night's rest first. In any case, there are no more coaches running to Brisbane until tomorrow.' Once more he indicated the car.

Lena's anger suddenly giving way to a sense of utter hopelessness, she seated herself in the front seat of the station waggon. What a beginning! But at least they had both spoken their minds. They knew where they stood. Or did they? It seemed that Rod Carron was not quite finished speaking *his* mind. When he got into the driving seat, he made no attempt to put the engine in gear, turning to her with an urgent air.

'What about my side of this obligation angle?' he demanded. 'If you felt you had to avoid robbing a poor old widower of six months' livelihood doesn't it occur to you that I might be feeling the same kind of complication? It wouldn't have been very kind of me to have walked off the property, letting it go straight to this New Zealand cobber, thereby robbing a poor little orphan girl of six months' holiday with pay. I understand you get your living as a shorthand-typist and live in London alone. It doesn't sound exactly bonza!'

'Widowers and orphans!' she said.

Suddenly they were both laughing — the kind of laughter which clears the air.

'Let's give it a crack,' he suggested. 'Six months on easy street at Windara. It can't harm either of us. And there's good old Mrs Clarens up at the house to play the heavy chaperon.'

'Maybe I could try it for a couple of weeks,' Lena conceded.

'Nice of you.' His tone was sardonic once more. 'But don't let me persuade you. I can clear out tomorrow if that's what you want. . . .'

As he spoke she seemed to look into an abyss, and she knew in a flash of self-knowledge that at the bottom of her heart the last thing she wanted was to turn tail and go back to the rather humdrum life she led in England. Already this green and gold country had put out its tentacles, drawing her to itself. Besides, she had more or less promised Mr McKindry she would give the peculiar project a trial.

She said, 'There's no need for you to go rushing off. I'll stay . . . for a little while. No more. Nothing permanent, you understand.' Her colour deepened beneath his quizzical glance.

'No wedding bells,' he nodded. 'You don't have to spell it out. Good old Tom may have known a lot about fruit farming, but he didn't know very much about human nature — and being a bachelor nothing at all about married human nature. What sort of set-up would a marriage be with the two people concerned forever suspecting that the opposite partner had come into it solely for mercenary motives?'

Lena felt an odd and wholly irrational chill at her heart at this cool summing up of the situation. Somehow it was the last thing she had expected. 'If you . . . if we . . . really feel like that would it be honest for us to hang about for the stipulated six months . . . or less,' she added hastily, covering her own possible retreat.

'Not in the least,' Rod Carron asserted. 'There's a lot to be done with the fruit during the next few months as we come into the summer and the stuff is all ripening, waiting to be harvested. I can't see this New

26

Zealand chap, who's some kind of academic, I understand, taking the job on at a moment's notice. And if the job isn't done and done properly it could lose the estate a great deal of money. It's a yearly turn-over, you see. We spend a lot on production and have to make that much and a good deal more in profit before we can declare it a viable concern.'

The words floated over Lena's head. She was fascinated at the way Rod Carron's face lit up when he talked of the work on the farm. He loves it, she thought with a twinge of pity. What a shame he was going to have to give it up. But that, she hurriedly reminded herself, was nothing to do with her.

'So if you can bear to stick around a while,' he was saying, with a glance of such eloquent pleading that it was more than she could bear. She wished he was not quite so good-looking, so persuasive. She hated the helpless feeling it gave her.

'All right, I'll stick around,' she conceded.

'Good girl!' There was that swift warm light in his grey eyes again. He touched her hand briefly — a gesture of commendation.

'Two gold-diggers,' Lena said, 'who aren't going to dig for gold.'

'If you mean you regret that . . .?' The sidelong glance this time was scornful.

Lena's temper flared afresh. 'For heaven's sake don't let's start all that again!'

'I'm not starting anything,' he snapped. 'Because it doesn't have to be started. It will always be there — suspicion. I told you.' With a jerking of gears he started the car and it went rocking down the rough track. The moment of understanding had gone. They were at loggerheads again, Lena thought hopelessly, and likely to remain in that unhappy state. How long would she be able to endure it? Thank goodness she hadn't committed herself to any specified time. If things became too grim she could always leave. All this stuff about the importance of harvesting the fruit crop had nothing to do with her. And anyway, why should they bother to safeguard profits for some vague New Zealander?

She saw with relief that they were turning in at a wide gateway. A driveway led up a steep rise to a two-storey house.

'It's very near the river,' Lena said, in some surprise.

'A quarter of a mile. I wouldn't have brought the car, only I knew you would have luggage.'

Lena scarcely heard him, looking about her with interest. It was a fairly long driveway. She had time to notice the well kept lawn, the wealth of brightly coloured flowers planted in formal beds near the house, which was built of weatherboard, painted white. It had the invariable Queensland roof of corrugated iron, painted a pleasant pale green. The house stood on eight-foot stilts so that cool air could circulate beneath the structure. A deep verandah, also roofed with the pale green corrugated iron, ran round three sides of it.

In a railed-off meadow to the left of the drive two ponies who were grazing looked up inquisitively as the car approached. With whinnies of welcome they trotted to the fence, hanging their heads over the railing expectantly. Rod Carron slowed down to call out to them. Something about the whole scene warmed Lena's heart — in spite of her reservations. Windara had a welcoming air.

'Billy-Boy and Melody,' Rod Carron named the horses before accelerating and continuing on his way. 'Mandy and I ride them when I have time to take her out.'

'Mandy?' Lena echoed.

'My seven-year-old daughter.' There was a note of pride in his voice. Lena glanced at his symmetrical profile. He looked too young to have a daughter of seven, his twenty-seven years gilded over by his bronzed tan. He couldn't have been much more than nineteen or twenty when he married — the tragic young wife who had died so soon. Had it perhaps been at Mandy's birth?

But they had topped the rise now and the car swung round into a roughly fenced enclosure, flanked by out-buildings. They drew up by a flight of steps which led to a back section of the verandah. Rod Carron helped Lena out of the car, took her case and preceded her up the steps at the top of which a wire-screened door opened to a small conservatory, its shelves laden with unfamiliar plants which filled the air with a damp fragrance. Like the tropical houses in Kew Gardens, Lena thought.

Beyond the conservatory, which was also a kind of porch, was a large kitchen with a spacious dining alcove at its far end. There was a smell of cooking and it was almost unbearably hot.

A gaunt-looking woman with faded grey-blonde hair turned from the stove with a cooking spoon in one hand.

'Mrs Clarens,' Rod Carron murmured, 'who looks after us. She was with your uncle for many years.'

The woman's dark eyes, fixed on Lena, held a glint of doubt as she summed up the new arrival.

'Miss Shannon,' Rod completed the introduction.

'How de do?' Mrs Clarens said mechanically, and in the same breath: 'Take the lady's baggage up to the big room, Rod. I've put her there because it's nearest to the bathroom.' She turned to Lena. 'We have no grand ways here, I'm afraid, I hope you won't find it too uncivilised. We have only the one small bathroom, one shower and one loo.' The explanation was offered defiantly.

If it's luxury you're looking for with your finicky English ways you'd better go elsewhere — she might have been saying — a defensive attitude Lena was to meet more than once. She had yet to encounter the mixture of jealousy and admiration with which many Australians regarded the Old Country — a legacy perhaps of the Continent's comparatively recent origins; the oldest land mass in the world inhabited by the newest of populations.

' I'm sure everything will be very comfortable,' Lena offered diffidently. Quite clearly Mrs Clarens wasn't altogether pleased to see her. But Lena supposed that was only to be expected. She was obviously in her sixties; no doubt set in her ways, and with the death of her employer her whole way of life would have been placed at risk.

' We have our tea at six,' she announced, as Rod picked up the suitcase and beckoned to Lena to follow him.

They passed through the kitchen into an adjoining room which looked like a lounge, though it was difficult to see clearly, for the windows were closely covered by venetian blinds. The same lack of light prevailed in the upstairs bedroom when they reached it. Lena, peering through the green gloom, made out a large bed, draped in mosquito curtains. Rod humped her suitcase down on to it and with a hurried, ' Hope you'll find everything you want — in what used to be my pad,' he withdrew.

So she had been given Rod's room, while he, deposed, had gone to live in a nearby bungalow — according to Mr McKindry. Would Rod and his little girl be eating with them? she wondered. Mrs Clarens had spoken of the six o'clock tea as if it were a family meal. It was now barely four and Lena would have been glad of a cup of tea right away, but she would never have the courage to ask the grim Mrs Clarens for it.

Tentatively she glanced around the shadowy room. It was airless and hot. She went firmly to one of the windows and pulled up the blind. The welcome light that poured in lifted her spirits. Why was the whole place kept so closely shuttered?

After she had been in Windara a few days she discovered the reason. The sun, here in the enclosed bush country, had to be kept at bay, and the heat of full summer would be a real enemy. So far it was still springtime, and yet the heat pouring into the house could be a menace. Unaware of all this, Lena felt she was doing the sensible thing when she raised the venetian blind. Instantly the golden blaze of the afternoon sunshine hit her. But the view beyond the uncovered window was breathtaking. This window, it seemed, was at the gable end of the house and it was not shut in by the verandah which shaded the downstairs rooms. It looked out over blazing flower beds and the green meadow where the ponies grazed.

In the corner of the field, quite close to Lena's window, stood a tall, broad-branched tree covered profusely with deep blue blossoms. They hung down like little bells from the bare branches, not a green leaf was to be seen . . . just this cloud of forget-me-not blue, and where the blossoms had fallen to the grass beneath there was a carpet of blue. Yet the tree seemed to be still supporting as many blossoms as it could hold. Lena gazed at it in fascination. It was, she thought, one of the most beautiful trees she had ever seen, and it seemed to be smiling a welcome. The only welcome

31

she had so far received. It was such a heavenly, hopeful colour. In an odd way it reassured her. In a world where such beauty blossomed there must surely be happiness! And it was here, close to her, so that every time she looked out of the window it would offer her its comfort. Tears filled her eyes. She dashed them away, ashamed of them. But her arrival in Australia had been such an anti-climax. Here she was, an unwanted stranger, flung into the lives of Rod Carron and Mrs Clarens with the strange terms of Uncle Tom's will trailing after her, a threat to their peace and security. Naturally they would resent her. But it was no use dwelling on it.

Shrugging her depression away, she turned to inspect the room. The furnishings were good but old-fashioned — the vast mahogany wardrobe, with dressing table and chest of drawers to match; the bed which was covered by a Victorian honeycomb cotton-fringed quilt was flanked by a heavy bedside cabinet. The carpet was good but faded. Clearly Uncle Tom hadn't spent very much in recent years in refurbishing his home, but being an elderly bachelor he would probably not have been interested in domestic details.

Unpacking her suitcase, Lena arranged her things in the beautifully clean, paper-lined drawers and capacious wardrobe. How many days before she would be packing them up again? This room which had been Rod Carron's would not hold her long.

When she had found the bathroom and had a wash and changed her dress her morale was somewhat restored. And still it was only five o'clock. Was she expected to stay in her room until it was time for tea? But that was ridiculous. Windara, if she so chose, was her prospective home — not that she did choose. But she had every right to be here and in a limited sense to take possession. Mrs Clarens must learn to accept her.

Confronting herself in the dressing table, Lena straightened her shoulders and took stock of herself. The hazel eyes looking back at her from beneath level brows saw light brown hair with golden lights in it, an oval face, small straight nose and a resolute chin, even if the eyes held a certain wistfulness, born of the moment's loneliness. She would go down to the kitchen and ask for that cup of tea, she decided resolutely, and bracing herself went downstairs. Mrs Clarens was busy at the sink.

'If I might make myself a cup of tea. . . .' Lena began diffidently. 'I haven't had anything to eat or drink since a snatched sandwich at the Brisbane coach terminal.'

Perhaps it was the nervous tremor in her voice which touched Mrs Clarens' heart. She swung round from the sink to wipe her hands on a convenient tea-towel. 'You poor child!' she exclaimed. 'Why didn't you ask for a cuppa when you first got in? Sit down there by the table and I'll have it ready for you in a jiffy.' She indicated the large dining table at the far end of the room, a beautiful rosewood table covered with a lacy cloth. A profusely blossoming shrimp plant made a gay centrepiece.

'This,' Mrs Clarens said, indicating the table, 'is where we have all our meals. We don't bother to use the dining room at the far end of the house. There's plenty of room in here and it saves trouble. No doubt,' a note of resentful apology once more crept into her voice, 'it's not the sort of thing you're accustomed to in your own home in England. . . .'

'My home in England,' Lena hurriedly corrected, 'since the death of my mother has been a London bed-sitter. I think this kitchen-cum-dining space is beautiful, with that lovely porch full of plants opening out of it, like a conservatory. You must be a very clever gardener.'

Mrs Clarens looked gratified. 'I'm not much of a one in the outdoor garden,' she admitted. 'Too many snakes about for my fancy. But I like my indoor plants.'

'Snakes?' Lena echoed in a small voice.

Mrs Clarens nodded with an air of gloomy satisfaction. 'Carpet snakes,' she said. 'Six foot long. Pythons, I believe you call them, and grass snakes and adders. You'd best be careful when you go into the garden . . . avoid the hollows where the grass is long and untended.' She jerked her head towards some back region away from the carefully arranged flower beds in the front of the house.

'Has anyone ever been fatally bitten by the snakes in the garden?' Lena asked nervously.

'Not while I've been here,' Mrs Clarens replied casually, as though fatal snake bites were a matter of small importance. She was pouring boiling water into a handsome silver tea-pot and a moment later Lena was enjoying a fragrant cup of tea . . . served in a cup of the finest china. There was a plate of home-made biscuits to go with it, but she limited herself to one.

'Best not spoil your evening meal,' Mrs Clarens agreed. She went back to her work at the sink, scrubbing small new potatoes, shelling peas. A basket of delicious-looking strawberries stood on the scrubbed working table beside the sink, waiting to be hulled. And under a wire cover lay a large plate of raw steak. 'Tea' was obviously a euphemism applied to the main meal of the day, Lena guessed.

'Won't you let me hull the strawberries,' she asked

34

when she had finished her tea.

'If you like,' Mrs Clarens conceded a trifle grudgingly. Clearly she wouldn't welcome too much interference with her kitchen duties, but a small task like hulling a dish of strawberries would hardly count. Lena watched her setting the places at the dining table, laying out heavy silver spoons and forks, small knives and steak knives. Peas and potatoes were bubbling on the electric stove. There was a delicious smell of fresh mint.

'Mr Carron and his little girl eat here, then,' Lena observed, eyeing the four set places.

'Of course they do! Where else?' Mrs Clarens replied. 'Lot of nonsense Rod moving himself and the child down to the cottage just because you were coming. This house has been his home for the past seven years. An agricultural machine salesman he was at that time and came out here to fix Tom Shannon up with some new-fangled equipment for the farm. But after the stuff was installed he stayed on, and has been here ever since. Took to the work on the farm like a duck to water. Your uncle thought the world of him, treated him like a son. I always thought he would leave him well provided for, but I never expected anything like the will he made in the end. Big upset it's been, for all of us.'

'For me too,' Lena put in. 'I had no knowledge of it, nor indeed that poor Uncle Tom had died until Mr McKindry told me when I arrived in Brisbane yesterday. It was a great shock to me.'

'Must have been,' Mrs Clarens agreed grudgingly, still obviously brooding over the strange will. 'I can't see it working out.'

'Neither can I,' Lena declared positively.

Mrs Clarens gave her a wry look. There was an

awkward silence for a moment, then she went over to one of the windows and raising the blind peered out. 'It's time they were home, Rod and Mandy. He went back to Latonga to fetch her from school.'

'All the way down the river again?' Lena exclaimed. 'Why couldn't he have picked her up when he collected me? Saving himself the extra journey.'

'He could have done on an ordinary day when the school closes at three. But today was the day for Mandy's afternoon ballet class.'

'Ballet?' Lena echoed in surprised enquiry. Ballet classes were about the last thing she had expected to find in the wilds of Queensland.

'Her mother was a ballet dancer,' Mrs Clarens supplied, and leaving this even more extraordinary piece of information in the air she began grilling the steak. A moment later the car could be heard coming up the drive and turning into the back courtyard. Then the wire fly-screen door of the conservatory-porch swung open and a little girl came running into the kitchen, followed by Rod Carron.

'I danced on my pointes today Mrs Clarens,' she began excitedly. 'At least, not quite on my pointes — I have to wait until I'm a little older. . . .' She broke off suddenly, aware of the stranger, and stood hesitant, a hand raised uncertainly to her lips. She was an appealingly chubby little girl, but her legs were the long graceful legs of a dancer. Unlike her father she had dark hair, cut in a bob to frame her round rosy cheeks.

Rod Carron put a caressing hand on her head. 'Go and say how do you do to the lady,' he suggested.

Lena held out her hands to the child invitingly. 'I'm Lena,' she said. 'I've come right across the world to be here with you, flying through the sky.'

'I know,' the little girl nodded. 'You came in an

aeroplane. My dad took me in a plane once to Sydney.' She had left her father's side and moving towards Lena held out a small polite hand. 'How do you do?' she repeated obediently.

Lena laughed. 'I'm very well, thank you.' She stooped over the proffered hand and dropped a light kiss on the little girl's brow. Blue eyes, which contrasted dramatically with the dark hair, gazed at her, solemn and intent.

'We had to go and live in the cottage because you were coming,' she said reproachfully.

Lena felt herself colour.

Rod Carron came to the rescue with a curt, 'That will do, Mandy. Run along and get washed for tea.'

Obediently the little girl departed. Carron stood a trifle awkwardly, looking after her.

'Didn't relish being turned out of her home,' grunted Mrs Clarens from the sink where she was pouring off the potatoes.

Carron swung round on her. 'Leave it alone, Martha,' he ordered curtly.

Mrs Clarens shrugged. 'Children always speak what's in their minds.'

'What's in all your minds,' Lena burst out. 'None of you want me here . . . trapped in a situation which was none of my making. But I don't have to stay. . . .' she ended, her mouth dry, her palms wet.

Rod Carron's grey eyes fixed on her were frosty.

'Of course you don't have to stay if you don't want to. We've been into all that. Do you mind if we have our meal in peace?'

Mrs Clarens had already put the grilled steak and vegetables on the table.

It was a delicious meal, but Lena could not enjoy it in spite of her hunger. For the most part they ate

37

in a silence broken only by Mandy's childish chatter. Twilight increased rapidly, Lena noticed, and suddenly it was dark.

When they had finished eating she wanted to help Mrs Clarens to gather up the used plates, but was firmly told to 'leave that, please, Miss Shannon. You go into the parlour and I'll bring the coffee in a few minutes, for I expect that's what you're accustomed to. For myself I always like a good strong cup of tea after my meal,' Mrs Clarens declared.

'Tea would do quite well for me if you're making it,' Lena said, feeling dismissed.

'You go along, miss,' Mrs Clarens urged, 'and I'll bring the coffee.'

It was pitch dark in the lounge. Entering it, Lena stumbled over a footstool and would have fallen if Rod Carron, coming behind her, had not put a steadying hand on her arm. As though she were a helpless invalid he supported her to a deep armchair, into which she sank, feeling oddly disturbed by his touch. He switched on an overhead light and taking a nearby armchair lighted a cigarette.

'You don't mind if I smoke?' It was more a statement than a question.

'Of course not,' Lena replied.

He offered her his cigarette case. 'I ought to have thought of this before . . . my apologies.'

But she didn't smoke, she told him. She could feel the heat from the overhead light adding to the already heavy atmosphere of the shuttered room.

'Couldn't we draw up the blinds and open a window?' she asked. 'It seems so hot.'

'It would let in the mosquitoes. I don't think the fly-screens in here are in very good shape. But we can have the small standard lamp on instead of the chandelier,' he said, and getting up changed the switches. The floor light was soft and rose-coloured. Crushing out the half smoked cigarette, he produced a pipe and proceeded to light it with due ceremony. The light from the match he used illuminated for a moment his lean tanned face, his brows frowning in concentration as he puffed the tobacco into full ignition. When he had got it going he leaned back in his chair, looking relaxed, gazing into space in a contented, withdrawn fashion which gave Lena the feeling that she didn't exist for him. Were they going to spend the rest of this strange evening sitting here in silence? Was he annoyed with her for her outburst at teatime? She would try to keep her disturbed thoughts to herself in future. Either she stayed at Windara, or she left. Whichever she decided to do Rod Carron didn't want to be for ever discussing it. She wondered how much of his time he spent here at the house.

As if sensing her thoughts he said: 'You don't object to my company for a little while, I hope. I'll be taking Mandy back to the cottage shortly and putting her to bed.'

'Of course I don't mind,' Lena assured him. 'In any case, you have as much right to be here as I have.' It was a remark that might have led to dangerous comparisons, but just then Mrs Clarens appeared with the coffee, served like the tea this afternoon in a solid silver pot. However careless Uncle Tom might have been about the furnishings of his home he had a nice taste in table equipment. All that solid silver cutlery on the dining table. . . .

There were two cups and saucers with the coffee pot, made of the finest china. 'You be mother,' Mrs Clarens said, placing the tray on a low table in front of Lena. 'Rod likes his coffee strong. I've brought a jug of hot water and another of hot milk so you can fix your own as you want it.'

'Thank you, Mrs Clarens. Won't you join us?'

'I've got my tea out yonder in the kitchen, thanks, and I ought to be getting on with the washing up.'

'Shouldn't I be helping you?' Lena suggested a little guiltily.

'Indeed no!' Mrs Clarens sounded shocked. 'That would be most uncalled for. You're the mistress of the house now . . . sort of!' she added in an ironical undertone as she left the room.

The coffee was delicious, freshly ground and heartening. Rod Carron went over to a handsome cocktail cabinet and produced a bottle of rum. 'Would you like a dash of this in your coffee?' he asked. 'Made from our own sugar cane.' He poured a generous measure into his own cup. but Lena refused to have any in hers.

'I didn't know rum was made of sugar,' she marvelled. 'Is that what happens to all your crop?'

'*Our* crop for the moment,' he replied, giving her a mischievous glance. But she wasn't going to be drawn.

'Most of it,' he went on, 'is processed in the ordinary way at a plant further up the river. It then goes as a rough product for further refining at a centre near Brisbane.'

Mandy, who had stayed in the kitchen with Mrs Clarens, now joined them, skipping into the room to stand in the pool of light cast by the floor lamp, her arms stretched out in a ballet dancer's pose.

'.Would you like to see the movements I learned in my class today? she asked, and without waiting for an answer pirouetted across the room to where there was a cabinet record player. The record that was already in

40

place was apparently one she knew. She switched it on confidently and the room was filled with the dulcet strains of the music from 'Swan Lake'. Pointing her toes professionally, taking up the classic posture, the little girl lifted her arms and began to move slowly and with grace across the floor.

Wholly absorbed and seemingly without self-consciousness she went through the stereotyped routine, giving it a childish freshness which was irresistibly captivating. Then reaching a passage where the music and the movements designed to accompany it became more complicated she missed her footing and stumbled. With a little laugh of embarrassment she ran to her father, who took her on his knee. She buried her face in his shoulder, saying in a muffled tone, ' I can't do the hard bit yet. But I'll get it right next time.'

' I'm sure you will, poppet.' Carron stroked the dark curly head lovingly.

Watching the father and child, Lena felt her throat contract. The fair head, bent with such tenderness over the dark one, gave the watching girl a sense of utter loneliness, a feeling of being shut out from a miracle completely outside her experience. A miracle which might never come her way. To hold a child of one's own in one's arms! She felt her heart grow cold and small in her breast, and once more she was remembering how alone in the world she was. Here in this strange house, thirteen thousand miles from the place she knew as home, her sense of isolation was almost unbearable.

She saw Rod Carron stoop to kiss the child nestling in his arms, his tanned, rather hard young face alight with fatherly devotion. He must have loved Mandy's mother very much during their tragically short marriage. A ballet dancer. How, in his

life as a machine salesman, had he met her? Lena
wondered.

CHAPTER III

When she woke the following morning Lena lay in a
half drowsy state, unwilling to get up and face the
difficult day ahead. For of course it would be difficult.
Here, safely alone in her room, the thought of it ap-
palled her. She shrank into her pillow and resisted the
impulse to pull the covers right over her head. As if
that would have helped her to escape from the inevitable awkwardness, or worse, which awaited her.

'I'll give it a week,' she told herself. 'One single
week — just for the look of it. Then I'll phone Mr
McKindry and tell him the situation is impossible and
that I'm going back to London.'

'Six months on easy street at Windara,' Rod Carron
had suggested. 'It can't harm either of us.' But it
could. Even putting it into words made it sound
mercenary and scheming. To embark on Uncle Tom's
stipulated six months knowing it wasn't going to work,
that they didn't want it to, was a kind of cheating.
Her only honest course was to have nothing to do with
it and go home. Home! A bed-sitter in Earl's Court.
By this time Deborah and Susan would have found
someone to fill the empty room she had left in the big
untidy flat. 'Third girl wanted' — she could just see
the advertisement on a postcard pinned up in the local
tobacconist's window.

With an aching sense of desolation she fought back
the tears, the sort of desolation it was wholly enervat-
ing and destructive to dwell upon. But from time to
time since her mother's death it had assailed her. At
such moments, facing her position squarely, she had to
admit that she was rootless, utterly alone in the world,

43

save for Aunt Dora who had her own two daughters to make the first claims upon her affection. It was only what was left over from family ties that could come Lena's way. She didn't really matter completely, vitally, to anyone.

And now, ironically, she had been offered a home and a husband, under the most unfavourable circumstances in the world. It was like a bad joke. But she couldn't lie here in bed all day beefing about it. Not that it was actually time to get up — the hands of her wrist watch showed that it was not yet six o'clock. However, with the desire to see what sort of day was dawning beyond the heavy venetian blind, she got out of bed, pulled it up and flung open the window. There was the jacaranda tree, a blue screen through which she could look out over the green meadow to the dense bush beyond. Billy-Boy and Melody were busy grazing. In the distance she could just catch a gleam of the river. Her gaze came back to the jacaranda tree. Its colour and beauty seemed to enfold her, comforting her, in a strange way banishing her loneliness. Only love, she thought, could have made anything so beautiful. Stretching out her hand she was able to reach the tip of one spreading branch and pluck a cluster of the bell-like flowers. Impulsively she pressed them to her lips. Trees and plants and all growing things, it was said by some way-out scientists, knew what you felt and were thinking about them, and responded accordingly. Was the blue tree really offering her comfort? Looking at the flowers in her hand, she experienced a sense of infinity in which all earthly limitations fell away. Peace filled her heart. A new confidence came to her and she was unafraid, so that when she saw Rod Carron appearing round the corner of the house she was hardly startled.

44

'Hullo!' he greeted her. 'You're awake early. It's only just six. I'm on my way to the cane fields. Later in the day perhaps you'd like to do a tour of them.'

She left the suggestion unanswered, wary of the eager response in her heart. What had the cane fields really to do with her? He was just being polite.

'Do you always start work as early as this?' she asked.

'Usually,' he replied. 'We get going early at Windara to catch the cool hours before the sun is fully up.'

Standing on the sloping ground beneath her window, he was close to the jacaranda tree, its lower branches spread out behind him. He was wearing a washed-out blue sleeveless shirt and white shorts, the invariable long white woollen socks pulled up over his calves. He looked very lean and tall, his grey eyes brilliantly alive in his tanned face. Lena became aware that she was clad only in a brief flimsy nightgown. Something in the way Rod was looking at her brought the swift colour to her cheeks. Hastily she backed away from the open window, with a murmured, 'Well, I'd better be getting dressed.'

But in fact she went back to bed. It was too early yet to start the day, which in this unfamiliar place would be long enough any way. And there was no sound of movement in the house downstairs. Mrs Clarens was obviously not about yet.

So Lena lay back on her pillows, looking out at the blue flowers and the blue sky beyond them, her thoughts milling around, her brief mood of peace shattered. She couldn't forget the look in Rod's eyes just now; half mocking, half . . . what? Oh, the sort of look you would expect from any man if you flaunted yourself before him in a flimsy nightgown. As long as he didn't imagine she had staged the little scene on purpose!

Before she met him at the breakfast table she had thrust the trivial incident aside. It was two hours later and she was hungry, enjoying the grilled ham and fried egg Mrs Clarens set before her. Mandy, eating cereal and mashed bananas smothered in cream, rejoiced that it was Saturday and there would be no school.

'Good!' her father said. 'That makes one less chore for me.'

'He has to take her down that river every weekday morning, wet or shine, and fetch her home again in the afternoon,' Mrs Clarens explained.

'Isn't that something I could do?' Lena found herself offering. 'I've done a bit of navigating at home. Last summer I went with two other girls for a week's cruising on the Thames.'

'You would be quite at home with our good-tempered *River Queen,* then,' Rod agreed quickly. 'She doesn't need much handling once you get the feel of the river. The currents are apt to be a bit stronger than the currents on an English river, I should imagine. But nothing to worry about in the ordinary way.' It sounded as if he would be glad for her to relieve him of the job of piloting Mandy to and from Latonga every day.

'Be something for you to occupy your time with,' he added.

'I don't think I shall be hard put to it to keep myself busy,' Lena said quickly, quite forgetting her re-action when he had suggested a tour of the cane fields. Now she was vaguely annoyed at his assumption that she would be idling about the place with nothing to do.

'I shall want to see all that goes on on the farm,' she went on. 'Get to know the various routines, meet the workers.' She broke off, suddenly embarrassed.

46

It sounded as if she were planning a survey before taking possession. But the truth was that she couldn't help being interested in this considerable property which Uncle Tom had placed within her reach. The very idea of it was such a fantastic change from being the humble tenant of a bed-sitter in London. But it was crazy to think of it like that. Her presence here in Windara was as impermanent as a dream . . . and as unreal.

'Maybe you would like to take Mandy for a ride on her pony this morning,' suggested Rod, still finding occupation for her. 'That is, if you do ride?'

'Yes, I have ridden a little,' Lena agreed, thinking of the decorous morning canters with the string of horses which were part of the routine at the Berkshire school to which her mother had sent her. They had lived in Berkshire before her mother died. The change to London after that had been dictated by the need to earn a living.

'Good,' Rod was saying. 'You can have Billy-Boy; he's an extremely good-tempered horse; in fact deplorably sloppy, always looking for caresses and of course lumps of sugar.'

'Billy-Boy is not sloppy!' Mandy broke in indignantly. 'Only very feckshonate.'

'He's a paragon of all the virtues,' Rod agreed.

'Don't say all those big words.' Mandy banged her spoon in emphasis upon the table. 'He's a good darling pony and I love him. But I love Melody too. Melody is *my* pony.'

'I haven't got any riding kit with me,' Lena pointed out.

'Good lord,' Rod laughed, 'those slacks you're wearing will do admirably. We don't go in for classy riding kits here. Informality is the order of the day.'

'I've got slacks on too,' Mandy pointed out smugly.

A little later the three of them were crossing the sloping field, Rod calling to the ponies who came trotting eagerly to meet them. They were both bays, with untidy manes not very well kept coats and white stars on their foreheads. Rod was carrying one of the saddles, Lena the other. The sun was mounting in the sky and beginning to make itself felt. Instinctively Rod led the way to where there was a patch of shade beneath the jacaranda tree.

Lena looked up through its branches, conscious once more of the strange effect had upon her. 'It's so beautiful,' she said. 'What do you call it?'

'Call what?' Rod asked absently, busy saddling Billy-Boy.

'This tree we're standing under. I can see it from my bedroom, like a great patch of fallen sky. . . .'

'Poetical little soul, aren't you?' His glance was quizzical. 'It's a jacaranda tree. They're very common in these parts. You'll see plenty of them.' He handed her the pony's reins. 'There you are, Billy-Boy is ready for you. Better give him that lump of sugar you've brought with you, and introduce yourself before mounting him.'

Lena needed no urging, fondling the pony's mane, rubbing her hand down his long muzzle. He nuzzled into her responsively, his rubbery lips closing on the sugar she held for him on her open palm.

Mandy was up on Melody now and Rod put out a hand to help Lena mount Billy-Boy. He took her whole weight for an instant as she swung into the saddle. For a moment their hands remained clasped. When she tried to disengage her fingers he held them firmly. 'Are you all right?' he enquired. 'Stirrups correct length?'

48

'Everything's fine,' she assured him, giving her hand a little tug. He let it go, but his intent gaze still held her own. It was an enigmatic gaze.

'Where are we going?' she asked. The question seemed to have a double meaning.

'I wish I knew,' Rod said softly, and Lena felt her colour rise.

'You can go along the track to the office,' Rod said then, 'and a little further along you'll find a path which takes you to the river.'

'The office? Do you have an office?' Lena's tone held surprise.

'Of course we have an office,' Rod told her. 'Where we keep all our records and accounts and correspondence. It's beside the cottage that Mandy and I are living in just now.'

'Why did we have to go and live in a cottage because you were coming here, Miss Shannon?' the little girl asked in a reproachful tone.

Rod threw back his head and laughed. 'Trust Mandy to bring us down to fundamentals!'

'Well, *why*?' Mandy persisted.

'To propitiate convention, propriety . . . prudery,' her father declared.

'I don't know the meaning of all those big words,' Mandy grumbled.

'You will one day,' Rod told her with a mournful headshake. 'Just thank your stars it's so much double-Dutch to you right now,' he ended, giving Melody a gentle smack on her rump. She moved off lazily, followed by Lena, who was concentrating upon getting the 'feel' of her mount. It was so long since she had been in the saddle. But Billy-Boy was as accommodating as Rod had promised.

'We go through the gate. I'll show you the way,'

Mandy called back importantly over her shoulder.

They came to the rough lane with the little railway track to one side of it. On the other side the trees and shrubs grew profusely; their stems and trunks half hidden by the long coarse grass. There was a pungent scent in the moist warm air. Eucalyptus, Lena realised. Eucalyptus was the name for the innumerable variety of gum trees which made up the greater part of the vegetation of the bushlands.

The ponies were trotting sedately side by side. ' Daddy doesn't like me to gallop, so I don't,' Mandy announced virtuously. ' 'Cept when he's riding with me. Then I can even jump a little bit, over low fences.'

It was a lonely scene that lay all about them. A bit eerie, Lena felt. The dense trees crowding so near to the track as if they were just waiting for a chance to advance and swallow it up. A primeval forest, undisturbed throughout the centuries — stretching mile after sun-drenched mile into the distance. Only the strange bird calls interrupted the profound silence. A kookaburra somewhere burst into raucous laughter, to be echoed by an answering mate. Flocks of small red and green parrots flew in and out of the trees, twittering to one another. Pink and grey cockatoos perched on the high branches, like feathery flowers. Galahs as they were called, Lena was to learn later. But for the moment she was wholly absorbed in the strange atmosphere of this primitive place. The pungent scents, the sights, the sounds, the burning heat of the sun, pouring down on to the unshaded track. . . .

She was glad when they came to a rise which took them up out of the valley on to an open hillside. Here she could see what must be the cane fields, acre after acre of close-growing sugar canes, the colour of over-ripe wheat and curiously stunted. She had thought sugar grew on long fully-leafed stems. When she asked Rod about it later in the day he told her the sugar cane tops were burned when the crop was ripe — to make transport easier.

In a hollow of the hillside were two cottages. 'The office,' Mandy explained, 'and the little house where Daddy and I have to sleep . . . because of you.' She was still obviously puzzled over the arrangement, and Lena didn't feel like exposing herself to a further barrage of questions about it. So she kicked her heels against Billy-Boy's flanks, urging him to a gentle canter. 'Come on,' she called to Mandy. 'Let's get to the end of this track and see what lies round the corner.'

They had left the hill and were on level ground, and soon they were trotting gently along the banks of the great river. It was greeny-blue in the morning light, widening in the distance to what looked like a great lake.

All at once they seemed very far from home. 'Maybe we ought to be turning back,' Lena suggested.

'I think we should,' Mandy agreed. 'Mrs Clarens gets worried if we're out too long. She says there are wild kangaroos and big snakes that climb into the trees and tarantulas that can drop down on you out of the bush.'

Lena shuddered, and quickly agreed that yes indeed, it was time they were on their way home. Later in the day when after lunch Rod was taking her on the promised tour of the property, she asked him about Mrs Clarens' dire warnings. They were driving in the estate car along a road which ran beside the river.

'Snakes,' he repeated, 'wild kangaroos and tarantulas. We can dismiss the latter for a start. They're mostly found in the corners of verandahs or outhouses and people are seldom bitten by them; they scuttle away at the sight or sound of an intruder. As for the poor 'roos, they're rapidly becoming more and more scarce. It's rarely that you see them in the bush any more — at least our kind of bush. They breed more freely in the wilds inland, the outback. Snakes are a more likely proposition, but even snakes aren't as bad as they sound . . . or look. The six-foot carpet snakes, or pythons, are quite harmless to humans, living on small animals and such. The copperhead and adder are not quite so harmless — in fact they can be deadly. But fortunately they're rarely encountered in the open and if they are they'll generally be more frightened of you than you are of them. If you stand still the odds are that they'll turn and glide away rapidly into the nearest bit of cover. Incidentally, avoid long grass when walking in the bush, keep strictly to the tracks. And if anyone should be unlucky enough to get a snake bite they should get to a doctor as quickly as possible. Meanwhile, the primitive remedy is to suck the venom from the wound. A pretty effective treatment, I've been told. In all the years I've been around in the wilds I've never had to prove it. In fact it's a hundred to one chance that you'll ever see even the shadow of a snake, save in some animal reserve or reptile zoo.'

They were skirting a plantation of sugar cane now. Smoke hung in the air and there was a sweetish burning smell.

'This is the burning off process I was telling you about,' Rod said.

A group of men were hacking at the canes which had already been burned, piling them into heaps. Rod stopped the car and hailed them. Two of the men came over to lean familiarly against the side of the car, one of them chewing a piece of sugar cane.

'Hi-ya, Rod,' they greeted him, then glanced

curiously at Lena.

'This is Miss Shannon,' Rod introduced her, 'boss Shannon's great-niece, who has come all the way from England to have a look at us.'

The two men nodded at Lena in an offhand way. Then one of them said, 'You're welcome, miss. The boss's death is a great loss to us,' he added sombrely.

'I left England unaware of it,' Lena found herself explaining. Why did she always have to say that when she was introduced to anybody? It was as if she were apologising for something.

The man chewing the sugar cane gave her a quizzical look, while the man who had welcomed her murmured something that might have been an expression of sympathy. But in the manner of both men was a veiled wariness.

'Do they know anything about Uncle Tom's extraordinary will?' Lena asked as they drove on after a few technical exchanges between Rod and the workers.

'Nope!' Rod shook his head very definitely. 'And I've taken care that they shouldn't know. There's a rumour afoot that you might be Tom Shannon's heir. But my part in the set-up has been kept strictly secret throughout the district — and I hope it stays that way. Only Mrs Clarens knows of my involvement, and she's discretion itself.'

'But she doesn't approve,' Lena pursued, perhaps unwisely.

'How could anyone approve?' Rod snapped. 'A suggested matrimonial alliance which breaks about every psychological law there is! Only a naïve old bachelor like Uncle Tom could have thought it up — bringing two total strangers together and flinging an ultimatum at them, baited with considerable financial gain.'

It sounded sordid put like that.

So what are we going to do about it? Lena won-dered. As though she hadn't already made up her mind! But somehow the events of the day had softened her resolution. The homely atmosphere of the house on the hill, the beauty of its surroundings, the lavish sunshine, riding with Mandy this morning, even the friendliness of the ponies . . . it all added up to some-thing that was very appealing to her in her loneliness.

And now the sight of the rolling cane fields under the cloudless blue sky awakened in her an odd sense of possessiveness, which increased as the tour went on. She saw the pineapple plantations, the strawberry fields where women in vividly coloured cotton frocks were busy picking. And whenever they stopped to speak to any of the workers she was given the same warm Australian welcome. They didn't resent her, she thought gratefully. If only all this wonderful estate and its activities could really belong to her! The pros-pect was a dizzying one. But the conditions surround-ing it were sobering. So was Rod Carron's grimly set face at her side. Beyond explaining to her the details of running the vast fruit farm he remained silent.

Was he too wishing the prosperous lands which they surveyed could be his own . . . without the ridiculous appendage of an unwanted wife?

On the way home he took her to the semi-detached cottage adjoining the one where he and Mandy slept. This was the office. There were well filled filing cabi-nets, a desk with a typewriter, and a basket full of correspondence waiting to be dealt with. Rod, pro-ducing a ledger from a safe, invited her to run her eye over the most recent balance sheet. She couldn't make much of it in the brief moment at her disposal and felt embarrassed perusing it in front of Rod. He would imagine she was gloating over the fat balance exposed.

So very soon she put it down as if uninterested, and turned to the basket of correspondence.

'Who sees to all this?' she asked.

'I do in my spare time,' Rod told her.

'But this is something with which I could help,' Lena said eagerly. 'I earn my living as a secretary at home, as you know. . . .' She broke off. 'So if you need a little secretarial help. . . .'

He gave her one of his searching, almost hungry glances. 'So you aren't taking the next plane back to England?'

She coloured at the mockery in his tone, but answered quietly, 'Not quite the next plane! I told Mr McKindry I would stay a reasonable length of time here and I suppose that's what I ought to do. There's so much involved.'

'Six months' lolly!' he taunted.

'I think that's a very offensive thing to say,' she commented coldly.

He was instantly repentant. 'I'm sorry. But you do tend to be a bit changeable. Last night you sounded as if you couldn't get away quickly enough, and that was after arranging with me that we'd give the set-up a try.'

'I know,' she agreed. And this time it was her turn to say she was sorry. 'Yesterday was a series of shocks,' she reminded him. 'I hardly knew what I was saying or doing. Today I've got things more into perspective. I could be quite content for a time taking Mandy to school by river every day, and seeing to the affairs in this little office.'

He shrugged as if it didn't really matter to him one way or the other. 'So be it,' he said. 'You're the boss.'

'No, I'm not,' Lena put in quickly 'We are the

boss.'

'A sort of twin-headed monster,' he sneered.

Her heart dropped and she felt her throat thicken. What was the matter with her? Yesterday she had only wanted to get away from Windara and never set eyes on it again. Then this morning as the sun rose she had fallen in love . . . with a jacaranda tree!

Mandy and the ponies, she thought; those rolling cane fields of burned gold. The colour of Rod Carron's thick blond hair. She caught herself glancing at it now with a strange hunger. She wanted to run her fingers through it.

But he was watching her with an air of impatience. There was a goaded look about him, as if he were driven by some indefinable force. 'We'd better be going,' he urged. He couldn't be quick enough, moving to open the office door. Standing over her as she passed through it he radiated suppressed energy. In the narrow entrance she brushed against him and felt her nerves tingle. They were both unbearably on edge, she decided, and wondered how long they could endure the bizarre conditions of their unsought association.

The next day was Sunday. Mrs Clarens announced at breakfast time that she was going to church and taking Mandy with her. 'Would you like to come with us?' she invited Lena. 'It would give you a chance to meet some of the folk.'

Without exactly meaning to ask his opinion Lena glanced enquiringly at Rod across the table. 'You might as well go,' he advised. 'It would give you a chance to try your hand with the boat. Mrs Clarens is a beaut navigator; she'll give you a few tips.

'Usually,' he added, 'I take Mandy to the beach at Doora Heads. But it's no day for surfing.'

The sky was mottled with racing clouds and there

was a cool wind blowing. Lena had been surprised on getting out of bed to find the temperature degrees lower than it had been the day before. But that, she was to discover, was how it was with the weather at this time of the year in Queensland — where it was still early spring.

'I'll be down at the office if you want me when you come back,' Rod told Mandy. Lena wished he had asked her to spend the morning in the office with him. He could have initiated her more fully into the business side of the fruit farm. But spending a couple of hours with her in the office was most likely the last thing he wanted, hence his anxiety to bundle her off to church.

It was still very early — barely eight o'clock. The service was at nine. 'We can leave the clearing up the breakfast things until we come home,' Mrs Clarens announced, hurrying away to don her Sunday hat, an imposing confection of artificial flowers piled on white straw. 'I'm afraid I don't very often get to church,' she confessed when she rejoined the waiting Lena. 'It's the new parson's first Sunday and we all agreed to make a welcoming congregation for him. But it's a long way to go,' she ended with a sigh.

Lena was glad of her light green coat as they boarded the launch. Mrs Clarens took the wheel as though to the manner born. The tide was with them and their progress was smooth. Half way through the journey Mrs Clarens invited Lena to 'have a go'. She took her place in the prow, grasping the wheel firmly, and felt the boat alive under her hands. Even going with the tide she was conscious of the pull of the strong currents.

When they passed Caloola Island Mrs Clarens told her the story of the hapless bride all over again.

'That rock in the middle gives me the willies,' she

confessed. 'There were strange goings on in the old times, from all accounts. Human sacrifices I shouldn't wonder. You can still see the marks on the stone where the sacred fires were kept burning.'

The church when they reached it proved to be a simple wooden structure with a gold-painted cross on the angle of its pointed roof. The service was short and simple, the familiar liturgy reminding Lena of her boarding school days. Mandy behaved perfectly, singing the hymns in a sweet little voice.

Afterwards there was a social gathering in the church porch. Mrs Clarens introduced Lena to several of the women who gathered around her. The congregation had been mostly composed of elderly and a few young mums with children. Lena found herself being warmly welcomed to Latonga, as Mrs Clarens explained her presence here. 'Mr Shannon's great-niece from London. He invited her to come for a holiday before his fatal seizure. She arrived, poor soul, not knowing what had happened.'

There were murmurs of sympathy and barely veiled glances of intense curiosity. Would this girl be part or whole inheritor of the Shannon fortune? The old man had seemed to be singularly without relatives. But manners were perfect and no questions were asked. There were several invitations to 'afternoon tea' — a light mid-afternoon tea break, Lena gathered, which had nothing to do with the full scale tea-dinner meal at six o'clock.

'Martha will bring you over to Coral Avenue,' a grey-haired little woman addressed Mrs Clarens. 'Won't you, Martha? Any day, just give us a ring.'

'She'll be finding it very quiet at Latonga and out at Windara after London,' another woman remarked. 'There's to be a dance at the Victoria Hotel next week.

58

Maybe you'd bring her over for that so she could meet some young people.'

Mrs Clarens made a doubtful noise. 'Dances aren't much in my line, I'm afraid. Perhaps Rod would take her to it.'

God forbid! Lena thought in secret panic. But she needn't worry. He would never agree to so intimate an expedition.

Back on the river they found the wind had dropped, the sky cleared and the sun pouring out its usual mid-morning radiance.

When they reached Windara landing stage Rod was waiting for them with the car. 'Thought I'd save you the walk up the dusty track in your Sunday shoes,' he remarked, as he ushered Mrs Clarens and Lena into the back seat, while Mandy jumped into the passenger seat beside him. 'Hope you don't mind,' he apologised to the two women. 'But Mandy always sits by my side when we drive.'

'Course I do,' Mandy confirmed smugly.

They had brought him a Sunday newspaper from the newsagent shop at Latonga and he sat in the lounge reading it while Mrs Clarens bustled about in the kitchen preparing lunch. Mandy was importantly dusting in the lounge.

'Let me help you,' Lena suggested. She hated sitting aloof like a stranger while the other members of the little household went their accustomed ways.

'You can do the mantelpiece and the top of the piano which I can't reach very well,' Mandy agreed, and ran into the kitchen to ask Mrs Clarens for an extra duster.

A peaceful silence followed, broken only by Mandy's humming softly to herself as she meticulously dusted the numerous knick-knacks on top of the long low bookcase. Some of them were beautiful tropical sea shells. Lena left her own task to admire them. Picking up a studio-sized photograph in a silver frame, Mandy announced in a tone of pride: 'This is my mummy.'

There was a startled rattle from Rod's newspaper, but he did not look up from his reading.

Lena took the photograph which the child held out to her. It showed a beautiful girl standing *en pointe*, wearing the classical ballet dress with calf-length skirt. Her hair was dark and there was a distinct resemblance to Mandy in her poignantly youthful face.

'She's very lovely,' Lena said softly, and handed the picture back to the little girl, who dusted it carefully and put it in its accustomed place on the bookcase.

Flinging his paper down with a goaded air, Rod rose from his chair and went out of the room, leaving Lena feeling illogically guilty.

'Lunch is nearly ready,' Mrs Clarens said, coming into the room. 'You'd better run along and wash your hands, Mandy.' She took the duster from the little girl, who somewhat unwillingly relinquished it. 'I've just shown Lena my mummy,' she announced.

Mrs Clarens' glance went quickly to the coloured photograph which now seemed to Lena to stand out like a light in the shaded lounge.

'Miss Shannon . . . Lena . . . thinks my mummy is very pretty,' Mandy went on.

Mrs Clarens sighed and shook her head dolefully. 'Run along,' she bade Mandy again. Mandy went. Going over to the bookcase, Mrs Clarens picked up the photograph. 'Dolores was her name, and wasn't it the right one for her, poor child, with her road of sorrow.'

'Where did she dance?' Lena asked.

'In Sydney. They have quite a good ballet company there, a professional one. Ballet is very popular in

Southern Australia. There are amateur ballet companies all over the place, and little schools like the one at Latonga. So it's easy to see how Dolores came to choose it as a career. She was just out of ballet school, working in the corps de ballet, when Rod met her and fell in love with her. He'd only started his job as an agricultural machine salesman with headquarters in Sydney and was making good money. Dolores took him home to meet her parents who lived out at Manly Bay near Sydney. They made him welcome, and the upshot was he and Dolores were soon married. Very soon Mandy was on the way and Dolores had to give up her dancing. A few months later she was gone, poor thing. A difficult confinement.' Mrs Clarens shook her head. 'All that dancing,' she murmured darkly. 'They must get muscle-bound.'

An 'old wife's' diagnosis which Lena doubted. People rarely died of difficult confinements nowadays. It was much more likely to have been an unsuspected heart condition or some obscure blood condition. Whatever it was didn't appear to have affected Mandy, who looked the picture of health.

'It was a terrible blow to Rod,' Mrs Clarens expanded. 'He left the baby with his mother-in-law and came out here with a big order for your uncle — complicated machines which he was supposed to stay a few days to install. Your uncle took to him at once and offered him a job as maintenance man and sort of overseer on the farm, or just some kind of general help. I imagine he must have told Tom his sad story. He hated Sydney after what had happened and it seems he told Tom he never wanted to see the place again. However it was, he settled in here. That was seven years ago. As soon as Mandy was any age, he brought her here and I looked after her. Adores her, he does,

61

and if you ask me he hasn't got over her mother's death to this day.'

At the sound of a footstep on the verandah she placed a warning finger on her lips. 'Never speak of Dolores to him,' she whispered, and fled to the kitchen as Rod entered the lounge.

But throughout the meal which followed he was unusually cheerful and suggested that as the day had cleared they might have a run to the surfing beach after all.

CHAPTER IV

The scene at Doora Heads beach burst upon Lena with the impact of a great orchestral symphony. Such colour! Such light! The ocean was a brilliant sapphire blue, shot through with jade, the breakers rising to a height of twenty feet to crash in a shower of sparkling white on the golden sand. Sunlight, rich as honey, illuminated the indented coast-line, which rose to a hilly eminence on both sides of the wide curving beach — the Doora Heads which gave the place its name.

On the hot sands a scatter of people lay sunbathing. But there was no congestion, no crowds. Children, well up the sloping strand away from the crashing breakers, played the immemorial childish games with buckets and spades. And there were the very necessary coloured umbrellas to shelter the half-naked bodies of the sunbathers from burning.

Sitting under one of the umbrellas, Lena watched Mandy playing nearby with some school friends she had encountered. But it was the surfers who claimed most of her attention. Clad only in the briefest of swimming trunks, their brown magnificent bodies suggested the perfection of Greek sculpture. Lena tried to keep Rod's corn gold head in view, but he moved so swiftly it was hard to watch his every movement. Poised on the crest of a great breaker, he would be carried shorewards at breathtaking speed, to be flung with his surfboard headlong into the boiling shallows as the wave retreated. The aim obviously was to keep upward on the slim surfing board, controlling it until the dry sand of the beach was reached. Nine times out of ten this proved impossible, but at the tenth effort victory over the wild water made the failures worth while.

They had driven from Windara in an elegant saloon car of Japanese make, which came as a surprise to Lena. She had been expecting the familiar estate waggon, but Rod explained that Uncle Tom had recently bought the Toyota. 'We use it for the odd trip into Brisbane, and when we go to Latonga by road instead of by river. It's a much longer way round, of course, but more comfortable in bad weather. And of course I use it if we go to Latonga after dark. By the way, there's to be a dance at the Victoria next week, Mrs Clarens tells me, run by the Rotarians. I'm a member, so I suppose I ought to put in an appearance.' He had given her a sidelong glance. 'Do you like dancing?'

'Yes, I do,' Lena agreed a little breathlessly. Why did her heart have to turn a somersault?

'Maybe you'd like to come with me, then. Give you another chance to meet the local residents. It won't be hard to find partners for you, I should imagine,' he ended cryptically. It sounded as though he himself would not be one of them.

She was sitting in the front passenger seat with him, Mandy between them. There was plenty of room for the three of them on the wide well cushioned seat of the luxurious car.

'Isn't Mandy bringing bathing things?' Lena had asked as they set off.

'She can't go into the water at the Heads,' Rod replied. 'It's far too rough. Another day I'll take you both to one of the quiet little bays the other side of the south headland. That is, if you care for swimming.'

'I love it,' Lena answered. 'And it must be marvellous here in the warm waters of the Pacific.'

'Dinkum,' Rod agreed.

When they reached Doora he had parked the car in a shady lot, planted with gums and palm trees. Then they had walked down the main street of the little town, Lena admiring the small luxurious-looking shops that displayed every kind of beach necessity from bikinis and surfing boards to umbrellas. Rod had insisted upon buying her the crimson and white umbrella under which she now sheltered. Then they had gone to a chemist's shop where he had picked out for her the best sort of barrier cream to protect her English skin from the searching rays of the sun. She was touched by his thought for her, but embarrassed by the amount of money he was spending on her. Prices were high in this choice resort and the cost of their few purchases had astounded her.

'Don't worry, it all comes out of the estate,' he reminded her. 'It's as much your money as mine. *Our* money,' he added, with cynical emphasis. She coloured. If ever money was the root of all evil! she thought wretchedly.

But the uneasy moment passed as they left the main street. As they climbed a rough path over a sandy rise the panorama of the great beach and the ocean burst upon them. Rod was carrying the surfing board he had brought strapped to the top of the Toyota. When he had settled Lena and Mandy under their umbrella he had slid out of his shorts and stood before them utterly without self-consciousness, clad only in brief trunks and his own magnificent tan. A moment later he was running across the sand, the surfing board under his arm, to plunge into the wildly moving water. Soon he was lost in the mountainous waves, where several other surfers were in action.

Studying the whole scene now with fascination, Lena noticed the man in a floppy linen hat perched on top of a high ladder looking out over the water with a pair of binoculars. In case any of the swimmers got into difficulties, she supposed. 'Is that man on the ladder a lifesaver?' she asked Mandy, who had not yet spotted her school friends and was digging a desultory hole in the dry sand.

Mandy gave the man on the ladder an uninterested glance and shook her head. 'The lifesavers always stay near the water's edge,' she said. 'There's one over there.' She pointed to a large muscular man, all but naked, guiding a group of little boys as naked as himself through a series of complicated physical exercises.

'That's my school swimming club,' Mandy explained with pride. 'For boys only. But they don't swim here . . . it's too rough. No children are allowed in the rough water.'

'And the man on the ladder?' Lena persisted.

'He's the lookout man, watching for sharks,' the child returned calmly.

Lena suppressed a shudder. 'Are there sharks about very often?'

'Only sometimes,' Mandy answered laconically. 'If one is sighted too near the shore a bell is rung and everyone comes rushing out of the water. It's very funny.' She laughed at the recollection. 'But they don't often come near . . . the sharks, I mean. Because, Daddy says, the fish they're after are mostly out further where the water is deep.'

It was at that moment she saw three little girls about her own age with the woman who was apparently their mother, settling down beneath an outsize umbrella, and darted off to join them. 'There's the Crowleys,' she exclaimed breathlessly before taking off. 'They go to my school. . . .'

Left alone, Lena became increasingly aware of the overpowering heat of the sun. Even the umbrella couldn't shield her against those penetrating rays. She stood up and slipping off her sandals stood barefoot on the burning stand. It would be bliss to walk over to the cool-looking wet sand at the edge of the sea. Where the waves broke and spilled over into runnels of shallow water. It might even be possible to paddle. She wished she had the swimsuit with her she had brought from England. She could have gone off and found the sheltered bay Rod had spoken of. A plunge into the delicious-looking blue and green water would have been heaven. But the thought of sharks deterred her. Best not try any experiments without consulting Rod, and anyway she had been tacitly left in charge of Mandy, she supposed.

'I'm just going down to the water's edge,' she called to the little girl.

'Don't go too far in,' Mandy counselled.

'Not likely,' Lena laughed, eyeing the crashing breakers.

A moment later she was standing with the cool breath of the sea in her face and the cold damp sand under her feet. She could see Rod more plainly now, every muscle of his superb body straining and working as he manipulated his surfing board. There were other surfers on either side of him, they came crashing forward, powerful, magnificent, expertly controlling every movement.

It was just at that juncture that the unexpected happened. The wet sand beneath Lena's feet caught her in a powerful undertow, threw her off balance, dragging her prostrate and powerless towards the towering breakers. In another instant the full force of the waves was all about her and she felt herself being carried out to sea in a smother of water and foam. It was all so sudden she didn't have time to be scared, being busy struggling to gain some control of her movements. But again and again she was tossed and submerged by the tide, as helpless as a leaf in that boiling cauldron of crashing breakers.

Then, just as her fight for air had begun to be painful, strong hands were dragging her free of the deadly pull of the current and she felt herself being lifted out of the water and carried on to the dry sand well above the water line.

Spluttering and drenched, feeling an utter fool in her clinging wet dress, bedraggled hair all over her face, she looked up into the calmly amused eyes of her rescuer. In a confused way she recognised him as one of Rod's surfing companions.

' What were you trying to do . . . drown yourself?' he asked. ' Or were you so keen to come to grips with the Pacific that you didn't even have time to take off your clothes?'

' I'm sorry!' Lena gulped, her mouth still full of sea water. ' That undertow, just now — I wasn't expecting it. It was like being carried away on a very rapid escalator, or one of those moving floors you walk on at airports. It just took me. I hadn't a hope and I couldn't possibly have kept my balance.'

Tossing the wet hair out of her eyes, she saw that her rescuer was a kindly-looking young man of medium height. He was looking at her with a mixture of amusement and tender concern.

' What on earth is going on?' It was Rod who had come to join them.

' I got sucked into the water,' Lena replied, feeling

like a drowned rat and an utterly foolish one into the bargain. 'Just standing on the edge of the sea,' she continued, her teeth beginning to chatter, not so much from cold as from delayed shock. 'I didn't realise the undertow could be so strong or come up so high on the beach. The sand just went from under my feet.'

'If I'd seen you. . . .' He broke off impatiently. 'Thank goodness Pete got to you before you were completely swamped in the surf.

'Pete Foster,' he added by way of introduction. And completing it the wrong way round, 'Lena Shannon.'

'Ah, the famous Miss Shannon,' Pete said, holding out a moist cool hand into which Lena put her own damp one. 'I've heard of you,' Pete was saying significantly as he squeezed her fingers in his strong grasp.

Just what had he heard? Lena wondered. In spite of Rod's assurance that the contents of Uncle Tom's will were not public property in the district she couldn't help feeling self-conscious when she encountered curious glances. Why had she come half across the world to visit her ageing relative and why when she arrived to learn of his death did she remain at Windara? These questions would surely suggest themselves and give rise to speculation and gossip.

Releasing her hand from Pete Foster's lingering grasp, she looked down at her dripping garments. 'How am I going to get dry?' she murmured. She was still fighting against a sense of suffocation which came from the water she had swallowed. A wave of dizziness swept over her. As she partly lost her balance she had the terrifying sensation once more of the sand slipping under her feet, dragging her under the breakers. Rod put an arm about her, supporting her.

'Steady on!' he encouraged her gently. 'I'll take

you back to your umbrella; you can lie there and dry out. If you slip off this wet dress you can wrap yourself in the towel I left there. I shan't be needing it.'

She was glad of his support as they climbed the gently rising stretch to the sheltering ridge of rocks and shrubs where the red and white umbrella awaited them.

Pete Foster had gone back to his surfing, she noticed. 'And I didn't even thank him properly for saving me,' she said.

'I guess you'll be seeing him again,' Rod hazarded carelessly. 'Sure you're all right?' he asked, as she sat down.

'I'm fine,' she told him shakily.

'You don't look fine,' Rod said. He stood surveying her a little doubtfully as she groped for the zip at the back of her dress.

'Here, let me do that,' he offered, and kneeling at her side unzipped the dress and helped her to draw it over her head. Why she should feel embarrassed at being exposed in bra and panties, she didn't know. She was far more closely covered than many females in the vicinity who wore nothing but the scantiest of bikinis. And Rod, wrapping the big soft towel about her, seemed quite unperturbed. She picked up the edge of the towel and began to dry her wet hair, meeting Rod's glance as she did so. He was on his feet again, looking at her in a contemplative way.

'You could have come to grief.' She was surprised at the feeling in his voice. 'And I didn't know what was happening to you. I ought to have been keeping a more watchful eye on you. . . .'

'You just didn't realise how silly I could be,' she helped him. 'But the sea looked so tempting. I only meant to paddle my feet in the shallows.'

70

'There aren't any shallows on surfing beaches.' Picking up her wet dress, he spread it out on one of the rocks to dry. How kind and practical he was being! The intimate moment warmed her heart. It was wonderful that he wasn't angry with her for her foolhardiness.

'I'm ruining your afternoon,' she said guiltily. 'Do go back to your surfing. I'll be quite all right now. This gorgeous sun is drying me out beautifully. I'm feeling quite revived.'

'Okay, if you're sure, then. . . .' With a casual nod he was on his way. She watched him with a sense of anticlimax run eagerly back to the spot where he had left his surfing board. That illusion of intimacy just now, of concern. He had done no more than the occasion demanded. Why should the thought hurt? What in heaven's name had she expected from him? It was Pete Foster the stranger who had seen that she was in difficulties. Pete, the stranger, who had come to her rescue.

She lay back on the hot sand and let the sun soak into her very bones, warming her through and through. Mandy came back from her play for a moment to give her a casual glance. Then noticing the dress hung out to dry she said disapprovingly, 'I told you not to go too far into the water.'

'I know,' Lena said drowsily. 'It was very silly of me.'

'Very silly indeed,' Mandy agreed sternly, and went back to her friends.

Closing her eyes in a pleasant lethargy, Lena found herself remembering a little too vividly the feel of Rod Carron's arm about her as he helped her up the beach, his burnt blond head bowed near to her own as she let her weight rest on his strength. If only he wasn't

71

who he is, she thought confusedly. If only Uncle Tom had never made that stupid will, creating a barrier between herself and Rod Carron which nothing would ever overcome.

The following morning the post brought two cheques from Mr McKindry; one for Lena and one for Rod. The peculiar payment for their presence at Windara. There would be one every month, paid in advance. Seeing the generous amount written on the slip of pink paper Lena felt once more the sense of unreality this whole strange business induced in her.

Rod waved his pink slip at her across the breakfast table. 'The bolt on the door,' he said. 'Neither of us can opt out now for at least a month.'

Had he been considering opting out?

'Easy money,' grunted Mrs Clarens, who apparently knew all about the conditions which bound them. 'Some people don't know when they're lucky.'

'Perhaps you'd better open an account at the bank in Latonga,' Rod advised Lena. 'You could do it when you take Mandy to school. And perhaps, too, you'd be kind enough to pay my cheque in at the same time.'

'Of course,' Lena agreed. 'And I'll go down to the office as soon as I get back . . . start sorting out some of those papers. Earn a bit of easy money,' she added with a wry glance at Mrs Clarens. 'And if I can help you in any way in the house. . . .'

'You can do a bit of shopping for me in Latonga,' Mrs Clarens said.

'Are you sure you can manage the boat all right?' Rod asked.

'She handled it just dinkum on the way to church yesterday,' Mrs Clarens answered for her.

It was a busy day which followed. The double

journey in the motor launch was a sheer delight, the river calm, the sun shining, the great birds flapping lazily back and forth. And Lena saw her first black swans.

Later, getting down to the office she spent a busy hour trying to reduce the piles of papers to some kind of order. After a time Rod joined her and they went through the backlog of correspondence together. It dealt mostly with orders for fruit and sugar cane.

'You'll find the routine acknowledgement of orders and assurance of delivery in the files,' Rod told her. 'Any problematical letters, complaints and so on, we can sort out together when I can spare the time. Right now I've got to get back to the cane fields where we're trying to decide which lots to cut first.'

She worked hard for another hour, then overcome by the heat which penetrated the corrugated iron roof of the little shack she went out to get some air. The door of the adjoining cottage was half open. Rod's hideout, the place where he and Mandy were sleeping. Impulsively she pushed the door open and found herself in what was obviously the main room in the place, half bedroom, half living room. There were two beds, both unmade. Garments were strewn about the floor in a haphazard manner. She longed to stay and put it all to rights, but Rod would be annoyed if she did. It was ridiculous to think of him and the little girl sleeping in this shambles when there was more than enough room for them in the house on the hill. The crowning irony seemed to be that she had been given his bedroom there.

She spoke to him about it when he came to the office after lunch to see how she had been getting on. 'There's absolutely no need for you and Mandy to pig it next door,' she pleaded.

She saw Rod turn away as she reminded him that Mrs Clarens' presence in the big house took care of the conventions.

'I'm not interested in the conventions,' he snapped back at her. 'It's simply that I prefer sleeping at the cottage in the present rather odd circumstances.

'And how do you know I'm "pigging it"?' he demanded after a pause. 'You didn't go in there, I hope?'

'I saw the door had been left half open and thought I'd better shut it,' she answered evasively.

He looked at her with suspicion for a moment, and then with a shrug let the matter drop. 'About these letters you've typed.' He indicated the neat pile. 'How are we going to sign them?'

They pondered the problem. 'You sign them. You're the one with the know-how,' Lena suggested.

'And you're the one with the name of Shannon,' Rod reminded her. 'This is known as Shannon's Fruit Farm, more often than Windara, and letters have been going out with the old man's name on them for years. Better keep it that way.'

So Lena, somewhat unwillingly, signed the letters.

The days of the week which followed fell into an inevitable routine, and like most routines the effect was soothing and reassuring. Lena was busy from morning till night, so that there was no time for painful introspection. By the time she got to bed she was so tired that she slept instantly. Her spirits rose. She began to enjoy life at Windara. There was a feeling of freedom about it, and increasingly a sense of belonging. She loved the daily river trips with Mandy, and working in the office; finding out the ins and outs of the fruit farming activities was fascinating. She was amazed at the amount of money involved, but much of it, she realised, would be used in running expenses, wages, fertilisers, the upkeep of machinery and the fuel for the sugar train which made its constant journeys to the processing plant. The processing incurred fees and so did the canning of the pineapples for shipment abroad. She was surprised at the high rate wages which were paid to the farm workers. Italians, most of them. They all seemed to have cars enabling them to get to the isolated farm from the places where they lived.

Often in the evening after tea, when Mandy had been put to bed, Rod would sit with her in the office, going over her day's work. She couldn't help noticing that her concentration during these sessions was not as efficient as she could have wished. The force of his personality seemed to dominate the little room, dimly lit at this hour by their not very efficient electricity; shadowy, intimate.

Why was she so anxious to have this approval over everything she did? Inwardly she despised herself for her weakness. But this effect upon her was something she could no longer deny. There was a strength and reserve about him, a hardness which intrigued her. He seemed so utterly self-sufficient, so unapproachable. Only with his little daughter did he unbend.

Twice when office work was slack Lena spent the odd free hour in the strawberry fields. They were situated on the level part of the farmland, bordering the river. The weather was ideal, the heat tempered by the slight breeze from the river. Clad in a brief sleeveless dress her whole being seemed to dissolve in the light and warmth. You didn't really need clothes at all in this idyllic climate. And the strawberries which she sampled were delicious. The pickers around her were friendly, mostly the wives of the workers in the cane fields.

With every day which passed Lena was more and more at home at Windara, more absorbed by all that it was coming to mean to her. In the office early one afternoon she tried to convey something of her feelings to Rod. She was sitting at the desk, one hand lying idly on the pages of an open accounts ledger they had been examining.

'It's all so marvellous here,' she began. 'Each day I find something freshly appealing about it.'

'Particularly in the accounts ledger,' Rod put in, a flick of ice in his grey-eyed glance.

Her heart faltered. 'What do you mean?'

He made a significant gesture, rubbing thumb and forefinger together. 'Lolly,' he said. 'Money, my dear. What else? You had no idea your uncle was so well cushioned, had you? It's bound to make a difference . . . no use denying it.'

She flushed hotly. 'I never even thought of it like that!' she burst out indignantly, and instantly knew that wasn't quite true. Of course she had been impressed by the extent of Uncle Tom's estate.

'Oh, no?' Rod's laughter was cynical. 'You wouldn't be human if you hadn't found the obvious prosperity of the farm a factor in your attitude towards Uncle Tom's will.'

'Do you really think that would influence me in any . . . ultimate decision I might make?' And why, she wondered in some confusion, had she used the word 'ultimate'? She had already made her decision.

But Rod was still grinning at her sardonically. 'Of course it must influence you. You've practically confessed that it does, by what you have just said. You aren't so sure now of the adamant attitude you were taking. Rejection of the terms of the will out of hand.

Now you speak of a decision in the future. . . .'

'I didn't mean it that way,' she began.

But he brushed the words aside. 'I warn you the season's prosperity is not likely to influence *me*. Save adversely. Can you imagine a union based on the financial benefits each partner was just waiting to grab?'

'Imagining unions of any kind is the last thing that is in my mind,' Lena returned indignantly. 'I'm here, as you well know, under pressure, for a limited period— certainly not more than the specified six months. I walked into the whole thing in all innocence. While *you* had every opportunity for leaving here when my uncle died, but you chose to stay on. Why?'

'You see!' Rod exulted. 'You're full of suspicions of my motives, and it's inevitable that you should be.'

'You're the one who started being suspicious just now,' Lena reminded him. 'When I was simply saying how pleasant I find it here. Can't I realise how attractive Windara is without your thinking I'm being mercenary?'

'No,' Rod returned unequivocally, 'I can't. And if this conversation doesn't show you how impossible any real sort of trust is between us, then nothing will. We're not living in cloud cuckoo land.'

'I didn't think we were,' Lena said sadly. Rod was right, of course; if Uncle Tom had wanted to erect a barrier between them for all time he couldn't have thought up a more effective way of doing it than by his unfortunate will.

She stood up from her desk. It was time for her to go and fetch Mandy, she said. She turned as she was leaving the office to find Rod looking after her with an unfathomable expression in his grey eyes. Was there a certain regret in them for the bitter things they had said to one another? She was imagining it, she told herself bracingly. Assuming a jaunty air, she said with a laugh, 'If we can't even go over the accounts without fighting maybe you won't feel like taking me to that dance next week.'

'Don't be silly,' he dismissed her suggestion. 'Nor were we fighting, as you put it, just now — just being realistic. And of course I'll take you to the dance. A date is a date. You don't have to dance with me if you don't want to. There'll be plenty of partners only too anxious to accommodate you — Pete Foster for one. You made quite an impression on him, by the way, during the romantic rescue scene. And incidentally, he's quite a well-heeled young man with a flourishing car sales business in Latonga. So if you're looking for a permanently cushy billet in good old Aussie. . . .'

'How dare you talk to me like this!' she shot at him, and ran from the room. As she made her way down the river her heart burned with a helpless rage against Rod Carron, and something deeper which she didn't want to explore. But all the beauty had gone from the sunshine and the swiftly flowing river. There was no magic any more about long-legged cranes who waded in the shallows. Even the little red and green parrots darting from tree to tree like flying flowers failed to exercise their usual charm.

For the next day or two relations between Lena and Rod were strained, Rod remaining cool and distant, Lena nervously ill at ease in his presence—a state of affairs Mandy's chatter at meal times helped to conceal. Once or twice Lena was aware of Mrs Clarens' perceptive glance going enquiringly to Rod's grimly set face.

'Something is upsetting him,' she said to Lena when

they were alone in the kitchen one day after an unusually silent evening meal. 'But he does get these moods of depression at times. It's no life for him, all these years on his own. Every man needs a wife,' she added with a countrywoman's directness. 'Though I doubt if he'll ever forget Dolores. As for Tom Shannon's clumsy plan to get him hitched. . . .' She shrugged her shoulders and laughed. 'Forgive me, my dear,' she added hurriedly as Lena coloured. 'But there is a funny side to it. Poor old Tom, he hadn't a clue about human relationships, or the way people tick. The last person in the world to go fortune-hunting is our proud independent Rod.'

'And it's not only Rod who's proud and independent,' Lena managed, gathering together the rags of her shattered dignity.

'I know, my dear, I'm sorry—sorry for both of you. For myself as well, for the will affects me as much as it does anyone. I don't suppose the New Zealand relative will want to keep me on.' She sighed and shook her head.

'All we can do is to take a day at a time and leave the future to take care of itself.'

An escapologist philosophy which didn't really solve anything.

Saturday came round again and Lena and Mandy went riding on the good-tempered ponies. On Sunday morning, instead of church, Rod took Lena and Mandy to the promised 'safe' beach, where they swam in the warm blue-green water. Rod, with his surfing board, made the best of the mild breakers some way out from the shore. 'What about sharks?' Lena wondered nervously, as she watched him. But the morning passed quickly and uneventfully. Rod's grim mood seemed to have lifted as he romped with Mandy in the shallows, or lay beside Lena sunbathing on the hot sands afterwards.

'Would you like to come to Doora Heads with me after lunch?' he asked her when they were on their way home back to Windara. 'See some real surfing again.'

It was the eagerness of her inner response to this invitation which made her cautiously refuse it. 'I think I've had enough sunbathing for today,' she told him. 'And I rather want to write some letters home.'

'So England is still home,' he said strangely.

She nodded emphatically. 'Yes, England is still home.'

CHAPTER V

Getting ready to go to the dance a few evenings later, Lena fought back the waves of nervousness which swept over her. She had bought a dress especially for the occasion at a smart little dress shop in Latonga on one of her journeys there with Mandy. For some reason she couldn't have explained she didn't want either Rod or Mrs Clarens to see her carrying the big showy box containing the dress into the house, and she had hurried upstairs to her room to hide it in her wardrobe.

Now, as she put it on, she experienced a thrill of pleasure. It was pure white, made of some flimsy, clinging material with the gleam of silk in it. Backless, it had a halter neck. The bodice was cut low, the skirt long and sweeping. Looking in the long mirror which formed one of the door panels of the wardrobe, she saw herself transformed, tanned shoulders and slender back attractively revealed. Her light brown hair had gleams of light in it, brought out by the electric bulb which hung over the dressing table, an uncovered bulb which had hitherto worried her with its need for a shade. One of the many little things about the house which had hinted at the kind of neglect which no feminine owner would have tolerated. Already it had occurred to Lena that it would be a joy to be able to put these small matters right. An impulse she had instantly dismissed as wildest fantasy. The short-comings of Windara House were none of her concern.

And now, at the dressing table, she concentrated on putting the final touches to her carefully applied make-up. As she had shaded her face under the beach

81

umbrella when sunbathing at Doora Heads it wasn't as deeply tanned as her arms and back and shoulders, leaving it a warm golden colour which emphasised the natural glow of her youth and health. The merest hint of eye-shadow had given depth to her hazel eyes, and the darkened lashes which curved above her cheek-bones seemed to emphasise the eyes' bright expectancy. But for heaven's sake, just what was she expecting? She pulled herself up sharply. Why was it that the least thing which happened to her at Windara seemed fraught with such extraordinary significance? It was as if everything which had made up her life until now had faded into nothingness. England, her childhood, her office job . . . even the loss of her mother and her home now seemed like a dream that had been blotted out by some violent awakening.

Australia, she concluded, had been a bit too much for her . . . travelling across the width of the world from one way of life to another she had lost herself.

It was simply that she needed time for adjustment, she told herself. With a feeling of suffocation she went over to the window, and pulling up the venetian blind, opened it. There in shadowy outline was her jacaranda tree, its colour just perceptible in the light of the rising moon. Not a breath of air stirred the bell-like blossoms. Picking a handful of them, Lena buried her face in them, breathing in their delicate fragrance. Then with a feeling of guilt for having severed them from the tree she put them in a glass of water on the dressing table.

'Are you ready, Lena?' Rod called up the stairs. 'We ought to be getting along. . . .'

Picking up the light coat which was to be her wrap, she ran down the stairs. Rod, looking up at her as she descended, audibly caught his breath. 'My! We have gone to town, haven't we?' was his slightly sardonic comment on her appearance. But his glance held open admiration—such frank and careless admiration that it left Lena with an indefinable sense of disappoinment.

'You don't look too bad yourself,' she returned lightly. For once she was seeing him formally dressed in a light grey lounge suit which seemed to make him look taller and more broad-shouldered than ever.

Mrs Clarens came to the door to see them off in the comfortable saloon car.

'Damn!' Rod exclaimed on the house threshold, feeling in his jacket pocket, 'I've forgotten the tickets. I must have left them in the glove pocket of the estate car where I put them when I picked them up yesterday. I won't be a tick getting them. . . .' He ran round the house to the garage in the rear courtyard.

'First dance he's been to for years,' Mrs Clarens said in a hurried aside as he disappeared. 'It's good to see him coming to life again. . . .' She looked searchingly at the girl in her beautiful dress and seemed about to add some further comment. But just at that moment Rod returned with the tickets.

The drive through the bush-lands in the moonlight was sheer enchantment; the silvery brilliance lighting up the pale stems of the tall gum trees and the shadowy blue-black of the undergrowth which surrounded them. They passed the sleeping cane fields—acre after acre of potential prosperity; coming out at last on to the bitumen high road where the big car picked up speed, so that all too soon for Lena they reached the outskirts of the town.

Throughout the journey they had not spoken and in the silence her nervousness had increased. Was Rod hating the prospect of the evening ahead of him? The first dance he had been to in years, Mrs Clarens had said. The first dance perhaps since his wife died. . . .

The Victoria hotel when they reached it was a blaze of light and a pandemonium of voices. 'Looks as if the entire population of Latonga has turned out,' Rod remarked in a resigned tone, as they pushed their way across a flower-decorated foyer—the scarlet callas and hibiscus almost swamped by the frills and furbelows of the ladies of Latonga. Beyond the foyer was a dining room in which an appetising supper had been laid out, and beyond that again was the ballroom, opening on to a large garden bright with coloured paper lanterns.

In the cloakroom where she left her coat Lena was greeted by several of the young mothers whom she encountered in her daily visits to Mandy's school. Their warmth and friendliness made her feel at home and accepted, easing the ache left by Rod's chilly silence during the drive from Windara.

'Your dress is a beaut!' one girl told her, and glancing at herself in a nearby mirror Lena couldn't help agreeing. Never before had she worn so revealing a dress, but it would have been a shame to hide that gloriously tanned back.

Entering the ballroom with two of her acquaintances, she found herself being introduced to an assortment of large deeply tanned young men, looking a bit constricted and uncomfortable in their conventional lounge suits. In no time at all she was out on the dance floor in the arms of one of them, frank compliments being whispered into her ear. But her eyes wandered restlessly, searching for Rod. She spotted him at last, leaning against the wall beside an improvised bar, a glass of some kind of drink in his hand. He was talking to Pete Foster, whose eyes raked the room until, encountering Lena's glance, he waved triumphantly.

As soon as the current dance ended she found him at her side, claiming the next number. He held her closely, his hand on her bare back clammy with the evening's sultry heat. Perhaps backless dresses are not such a good idea in this climate, she thought wryly.

'It's suffocating in here, let's go into the garden for a breath of air,' Pete suggested presently. Guiding her through an open French window, he led her on to a wide verandah. Steps led down into the moonlit garden, where flowers bloomed in profusion, branching poinsettia, coral trees, bottlebrush trees, roses. The air was heavy with the dew-wet fragrance of the growing things, grass and trees and flowers alike.

Halting in the shadow of a cluster of date palms, Pete turned to her. 'In this moonlight, in your white dress, you don't look real,' he whispered. 'A dream girl. Oh, Lena, you're so lovely. . . .' His hands rested lightly on her shoulders. Involuntarily she shrank from him.

'It's all right,' he assured her. 'I'm not going to pester you. I think far too much of you for that.' His voice was not quite steady. She looked up into his frank, kindly face and her heart warmed to him.

'You're nice, Pete,' she said. 'And you *did* rescue me from the breakers the other day, didn't you?' On an impulse she leaned forward and touched his cheek lightly with her lips—a crazy thing to do, for of course his arms were around her instantly and he was kissing her purposefully.

'No, Pete!' she gasped. 'Mine was just a little "thank you" kiss. I didn't mean anything . . . like this. . . .'

But it was too late, he was burying his lips in her hair, whispering extravagant words of love. And it was just at that moment, looking over Pete's shoulder, that Lena saw Rod standing on the verandah watching them, moonlight and lantern light revealing them. As she made a vain attempt to disentagle herself from Pete's embrace, Rod turned on his heel and walked back into the ballroom.

'No, Pete, no!' she pleaded again, and with a final effort broke away from him.

'I'm sorry, Lena!' He was all penitence at once. Smoothing back his ruffled locks, straightening his tie, he regarded her ruefully. 'You shouldn't be so beautiful. It's more than flesh and blood can stand!'

They were walking back to the verandah. 'I didn't mean to go for you like that,' he continued to apologise. 'Now I've mucked up everything between us. . . .'

There wasn't anything between us, she wanted to point out, but it would have sounded so heartless. Instead she said carelessly, 'Forget it, Pete. It didn't mean a thing.'

'Not to you, perhaps,' he muttered forlornly.

They were back in the glare and noise of the dancing now and another partner claimed her. Was he one of the men to whom she had been introduced when she arrived? She couldn't remember. They all looked so alike, these big tanned Australians. Except Rod with his thick dark-gold hair and air of aloofness. Wasn't he ever going to dance with her? Wasn't he going to dance with anybody? For he was still propping up the improvised bar, talking with the casual drinkers who joined him and drifted away again.

It was half way through the evening before he came to her and asked her if she would like some supper. There had been a general movement towards the buffet in the dining room. Lena went along with him, glad of the ice-cold pineapple drink he found for her, but she had little appetite for the delicious 'eats'. Toying

86

with a crab and mango patty, she watched Rod dispose of delicacy after delicacy. 'Jolly good tuckers!' he commended it. In the adjoining ballroom the orchestra had struck up again.

'Don't you ever dance?' she asked him at last in desperation.

He shrugged. 'It's been so many years since I took the floor that I'm a bit doubtful of my ability. If you wouldn't mind risking it . . .?'

'Of course not!' She tried to keep the eagerness out of her voice. Unluckily it was a swinging number, and Rod looked at the gyrating figures in some bewilderment. Then as if deciding to dismiss them he put an arm firmly about Lena's waist and swung her into a gentle waltz step which bore little relation to the tempo of the pop tune the band was playing. 'All that head-wagging and arm-waving,' he mocked. 'Not my line of country at all. I'm all for the old-fashioned dances . . . hope you don't mind. If you'd rather have this one with Pete. . . .'

'Oh, no!' she interrupted a little too hurriedly. Every bone in her body seemed to have melted at his touch.

I'm in love with him, she thought despairingly. And what a time and place in which to discover it! The shock of it ran through her like a physical pain. It wasn't merely his nearness, the feel of his arms around her—carefully kept at her waistline. No hands on bare backs for Rod! He would never make a cheap thing of casual moments on a dance floor. He was too direct, too honest. But if he had really loved her. . . . She broke away from the thought, overwhelmed by its implications. Crazy thoughts. Let her stick to reality. The reason he was holding her so impersonally was that he wasn't particularly interested in her. She looked

87

up at him, meeting his enigmatic but oddly weary glance.

'You're not enjoying this, you look worried,' he said, and firmly marched her off the floor to a palm-filled alcove where Pete Foster was eagerly waiting for her.

'You take her, Pete,' Rod said as he handed Lena over. 'She doesn't like my kind of dancing, and I can't say I blame her.'

After that the evening went its predictable way, with Lena being passed from partner to partner—when she wasn't dancing with Pete, which happened as often as Pete could work it. It was well into the small hours when Rod came to her and said it was time they were going home.

'If you can tear yourself away from Pete!' It was spoken with a certain truculence which might have implied that he was disturbed by her growing friendship with Pete Foster. But she couldn't believe it was so. It was far more likely that he had had a bit too much to drink in his effort to overcome the long hours of boredom, and he had wanted to needle her.

She let the remark pass. It would be stupid to start arguing about Pete Foster, who meant so little to her, and anyway Rod was hurrying her from the hotel, giving her no time at all for farewells to her retinue of obvious admirers.

The moon had gone down by now and the night was black and hot beyond the headlights of the car. Wasn't Rod driving rather recklessly? They seemed to be bumping along at a terrific rate over the dirt roads in the bushlands. And once more conversation was kept to a minimum. Until Rod said coldly, 'I hope you enjoyed yourself tonight. You seemed to be having a great success with the chaps. . . .'

'It was a good dance,' she agreed wearily.

'Dinkum is the word,' he told her. 'Fair dinkum! If you're going to settle in Australia you'd better learn some Australianese.'

'What makes you think I'm going to settle in Australia?' she asked, startled.

He laughed dryly. 'It must surely be beginning to dawn on you that Windara isn't the only option. Pete would lay his life and all his worldly goods at your feet tomorrow, if you gave him the least encouragement.'

'Australian beer talking,' she mocked.

'The best beer in the world,' he declared, in a tone which defied contradiction. 'And the strongest. And don't forget that " when wine is in truth is out ". I know I've had one or two over the eight, but I had to do something to while away the endless hours.'

'I'm sorry you had to suffer so much on my behalf. We could have come away earlier.'

'No. we couldn't. You were the belle of the ball and I hadn't the heart to break it up. If you don't want Pete there are plenty of other guys who would gladly step into his shoes.'

A postulation too silly to discuss, she decided. And anyway, they were turning in at the gateway of Windara House. They stood by the front door on the verandah while Rod fumbled for the key. When he had fitted it into the lock he turned to her and to her complete surprise threw an arm about her shoulder, drew her roughly towards him, and planted a kiss full on her lips. 'The classic finale to an evening out with a pretty girl,' he said. 'Salute to Eros or whoever it was. . . .' The words trailed away indistinctly.

'You're drunk!' Lena accused him inexcusably, and with an angry 'Goodnight' ran into the house and up the stairs to her room. The kiss which had been more of an insult than a caress burned on her lips. Her heart beat unevenly. She stood still with her hands to her face listening to Rod putting the car away before he departed for the lonely little cottage in the valley, where tonight not even Mandy would be waiting for him. She was sleeping in Mrs Clarens' room since it would have been unwise to leave her alone in the cottage while Rod went to the dance.

The garage doors banged noisily. Rod's footsteps retreated down the drive, echoing through the profound silence of the night. On an irresistible impulse Lena went to her window and drawing up the blind looked out. Perhaps a moment of communion with her jacaranda tree would still the tumult within her. It stirred in its sleep as, opening the window, she leaned towards it—the movement, mysterious in the windless night, was oddly comforting. Away to the east there was a red glow in the sky. Surely it couldn't be the dawn yet? It was barely three o'clock. She could hear somebody running along the track beyond the property boundary. Rod? In the darkness she couldn't make out in which direction he was going. But it seemed to be away from the cottage. There was beginning to be a faintly acrid smell in the air. Something was on fire somewhere. And even as the unwelcome possibility dawned on her the dull red glow turned into a great gush of flame which shot up into the sky, illuminating the surrounding landscape.

A bush fire! she realised in horror—the culmination of this week of intense heat. She had heard of bush fires, but never expected to encounter one, imagining they only happened away in the Outback, safely away from civilisation.

For a moment she stood paralysed, then she ran

along the corridor to Mrs Clarens' door and knocked on it softly. There was no response. She knocked again and this time pushed the door ajar. 'Mrs Clarens!' she called.

With an exclamation of alarm Mrs Clarens sat up in her bed and switched on the light. 'What is it?' she enquired sharply, none too pleased to having been summarily aroused.

'A fire,' Lena told her breathlessly. 'The whole sky is lit up with it. It looks as if it's somewhere on the border of the property . . . at the top of the hill where the cane fields are.'

Mrs Clarens was out of bed in an instant, pushing her arms into the sleeves of a shabby dressing gown. In the cot bed by her side Mandy slept peacefully.

'Does Rod know?' Mrs Clarens asked.

'I think so. He'd just left me here at the house and I heard him running in the direction of the fire.'

Mrs Clarens drew up her blind. Billows of smoke shot through the flames which filled the eastern sky.

'When it gets hold of the bush it leaps all the fire-breaks,' she pronounced in a flat tone of despair. She passed her hand across her brow. 'Such a time of night for it to happen!' She peered at her bedside clock. 'It's not going to be easy to rouse the fire-fighters.'

'Do they come from Latonga?' Lena asked.

'From everywhere. The neighbours, the workers on the farm, the fire brigade from Latonga, they all join in. By the time the fire gets a real hold it will be visible for miles around and they'll all come running . . . if it isn't too late!

'At least there's no wind to fan the flames.' She turned from the window. 'We'd better get dressed.' She glanced at Lena in her dance dress. 'Anyway, I had,

91

and if I were you I'd change into something more practical. We'll go down to the kitchen and put on all the kettles we can find. There may be casualties. In any case, the men when they come in will be glad of tea . . . gallons of it.'

Back in her own room Lena found herself trembling. Beneath Mrs Clarens' forced calm she had sensed extreme tension. How did they stop these raging bush fires? She pushed the question away from her and turning her back to the window with its terrifying glimpse of smoke and flame took off her dress and slipped on a pair of slacks and a pullover. When she went downstairs Mrs Clarens, fully dressed, was out on the verandah, gazing away into the angry red glow. The air was heavy with the smell of burning gum trees —the pungent odour of eucalyptus. The fire seemed to be nearer, creating a false and violent dawn which illuminated the garden with its flowers, the paddock where the ponies had begun to graze, apparently undisturbed as yet by the strange light and heat. Lena could feel the warmth on her face. Could the fire reach the hill on which the house stood?

As if reading her thoughts Mrs Clarens said, ' We're safe enough here, my dear. The creek which runs from the river, skirting the cane fields will stop the flames spreading in this direction. I remember the last time it happened, ten years ago. . . .' She broke off as if unwilling to pursue the grim recollection.

' It's on the side away from the creek the men will be cutting the fire breaks and digging the ditches. They beat the flames down with wet sacks . . . the creek is a godsend.'

The lights of cars were flashing along the distant high road now, and far away Lena could hear the strident ringing of a fire bell.

They went into the house and sat silently in the kitchen where the kettles of boiled water waited. Mrs Clarens had produced a large box of first aid appliances. 'It's not only from burns they suffer,' she said, 'but hands badly blistered from all the digging, strained muscles from digging out the tree roots, and their eyes become half blinded by the smoke.'

It was ominously quiet as they waited. Would the dawn never come? Lena had an all too vivid picture of Rod in his trim lounge suit fighting the flames. What was happening to him at this moment? She covered her face with her hands.

Mrs Clarens eyed her with concern. 'Don't let yourself think about it, Lena. The men will be all right. They're used to coping with these bush fires every so often.' But she didn't sound wholly convinced. A moment later she was making a pot of tea. 'We'd better fortify ourselves while we're waiting,' she advised.

It was as they were drinking the welcome tea that the first great clap of thunder rent the air. Mrs Clarens sat arrested, her tea cup poised in the air. 'Thank God!' she breathed. 'If we could get a really good storm it could save the day.'

Even as she spoke the thunder rolled again, a prolonged crashing and tumbling sound as though the very heavens were caving in.

'So it was thunder clouds making the night so long, keeping the daylight back,' Mrs Clarens decided, going to peer out of the window as great, crackling flashes of lightning lit up the whole sky. And almost at once the rain began to fall. It fell in solid sheets, sluicing down with the impact of a waterfall so that the whole world was filled with its tumult.

'It's a miracle!' Mrs Clarens whispered, tears of

gratitude rolling down her lined cheeks.

During the half hour which followed the rain came down steadily. The driveway from the house became a river, the lower part of the paddock a pond. Huddled together, the ponies looked wet and forlorn in the first grey light of day.

'But the water will soon drain away,' Mrs Clarens said. 'We're lucky here on our hill top. One hot day and we'll be dried out again.' She had been upstairs to find Mandy sleeping peacefully through all the turmoil. 'What it is to be young!' she sighed as she spoke to Lena of the sleeping child.

Soon after that the first of the fleet of cars began to arrive at the house—jeeps, estate cars, cars large and small disgorging their loads of exhausted men. Led by Rod they came into the house, at least a score of them; filling the kitchen and the lounge. Weary giants with smoke-blackened faces. The completely sobered Rod with singed hair and eyebrows was barely recognisable: his trim suit ruined with smoke, fire-ash and rain.

There were burned hands to be bandaged, as Mrs Clarens had foreseen. One man had a badly sprained ankle, another had almost dislocated his shoulder heaving trees out of the path of the flames. Mrs Clarens did most of the dressings, while Lena poured numerous cups of tea laced liberally with rum. No one seemed inclined to talk very much. To Mrs Clarens' anxious, 'How much damage have we got?' there was a chorus of brief unprintable comments.

'We've lost most of the cane on the eastern slopes,' Rod provided grimly.

The thunder had ceased now and the rain was abating. Mrs Clarens was frying great pans of bacon and eggs, while Lena made more tea. It was eight o'clock when the men, having eaten and rested, went on their way, thanking the women for their ministrations.

'It's all of you who should be thanked,' Mrs Clarens returned. 'Coming out here in the dead of night, heedless of the miles and the danger, risking your lives to save our property.'

'Anyone would do the same for a mate,' one man asserted, putting an arm about Rod's shoulder.

Mrs Clarens nodded. 'Mateship,' she agreed. 'That good old word living on from the past, when it was mateship which made Australia what she is today. And it's still our standby in times of crisis.'

There was an embarrassed silence at this idealistic pronouncement.

It was only when they had all departed that Rod revealed his badly lacerated palms. Mrs Clarens had gone upstairs to help Mandy to dress and Lena was alone with him in the kitchen, starting to clear up the confusion left by used breakfast dishes and first aid equipment.

'Do you think you could find some bandages for these?' Rod asked, holding out his bleeding hands.

Lena took them in her own with a small exclamation of dismay. 'Oughtn't they be bathed in some kind of antiseptic?'

'Probably,' Rod shrugged.

Lena fetched a basin half filled with warm boiled water laced with some of the disinfectant lotion Mrs Clarens had been using. Washing Rod's wounded hands in this mixture she wouldn't let herself think of anything but the dressing she was applying. This intimate little task must be taken impersonally . . . no upsurging of selfish emotions. Rod was suffering . . . and exhausted.

'You ought to go to bed,' she told him.

95

But he shook his head. There was too much to see to on the cane fields. 'I'll have to change first,' he said. 'If I could only have a bath—but that's impossible with these bandaged hands. Perhaps you could wipe some of the smoke and dirt off my face.'

She fetched another basin of warm water, with eau de cologne in it this time. Rod, now leaning back in one of the armchairs in the lounge, closed his eyes while she gently sponged his scorched brow.

Presently, opening his eyes, he smiled up at her. 'You do it so beautifully,' he told her. 'You have the lightest touch. You wouldn't willingly hurt anyone, would you, Lena?'

'Of course not!' What a strange thing to say.

But his eyelids drooped even as he spoke and in a moment he was asleep. He slept there in the armchair for a good two hours, while Lena and Mrs Clarens crept about the house careful not to waken him. It was explained to Mandy too that she must be 'quiet as a little mouse', playing with her jigsaw puzzle at the end of the dining table in the kitchen alcove. There could be no journey down the flooded river to school today. Mrs Clarens told her about the bush fire which had kept her father out half the night. But she made as light of it as possible.

'Why are Daddy's hands bandaged, then?' Mandy whispered with a glance towards the opening to the lounge where Rod still slept.

'He hurt them digging up the trees to make fire breaks,' Mrs Clarens told her.

Mandy nodded. Apparently she knew all about fire breaks, and continued with her jigsaw puzzle in obedient silence.

CHAPTER VI

When Rod woke up he seemed a bit dazed and inclined to be short-tempered. Coming into the kitchen, where Lena was still helping Mrs Clarens with the disrupted household tasks, he enquired testily why Mandy had not gone to school.

'Because of the bush fire,' the little girl supplied abstractedly, still engrossed in her puzzle.

'The river may be running high after last night's heavy rain,' Mrs Clarens reminded him. 'I thought it would be too much for Lena, handling the launch in these circumstances.'

'I suppose so.' Rod gave Lena a withering glance. 'I'll take Mandy myself after lunch, in time for the afternoon session, then I can get a proper dressing from the doctor for these blasted hands. I can't do a thing muffled up in these bandages.'

'Maybe a few strips of adhesive plaster would be better,' Mrs Clarens suggested, and rummaging in the first aid box, which she had not yet put away, she found the dressings she was looking for.

Adhesive plaster. Why hadn't she thought of that? Lena reproached herself.

Flexing his palms, Rod looked down at the fresh covering with approval. 'Now I can change out of this filthy suit. I'll take it to the cleaners this afternoon. Meanwhile I'll slip down to the cottage and change into more suitable gear.

'Would you like to come with me and have a look at the office?' he asked Lena. 'I hope the rain hasn't done too much damage, but I'm afraid the roof is not exactly weatherproof.'

'Neither is the roof of the cottage next door,' Mrs Clarens reminded him. 'Why you imagine you have to go on sleeping down there instead of in your own comfortable room up here. . . .' She broke off with a baffled gesture.

So Mrs Clarens too found his avoidance of Windara House a little odd, Lena noticed.

'I've *told* you,' Rod was saying impatiently. 'I like it down there.'

'Okay,' Mrs Clarens agreed drily. 'But you don't have to keep Mandy down there with you. For one thing, it makes very awkward evenings for you, having to stay down there with her after she's been put to bed.'

'I do my office work then,' Rod said.

Mrs Clarens, ignoring the interruption, went on with her plea: 'She was perfectly all right with me last night. Or I could easily fix up the little spare room for her. It's right beside my room and I could keep the communicating door open so that she wouldn't be nervous.'

Rod, assuming his most obstinate air, left this suggestion unanswered.

'Are you coming with me?' he asked Lena tersely.

They went out into the rain-wet world, steaming now in the morning's heat and sunshine. Lena glanced anxiously at her jacaranda tree. It was still blue and beautiful, but many of the blossoms had been knocked off by the force of the rain and lay in a thick blue carpet on the grass beneath.

Rod limped a little as he walked beside her—a strained leg muscle, perhaps. Mrs Clarens had said strains were one of the hazards of clearing the ground in the path of the advancing fire. Just what had he been through last night? She glanced at his grim profile and as if conscious of her scrutiny he turned and glared at her. 'I suppose you realise,' he shot at her, 'that we've lost about a third of the season's cane crop in last night's fire. One part of the hill is a blackened ruin. Come and look at it.'

He led the way up a winding path which took them above the valley where the two cottages were situated. The sight that awaited them made Lena catch her breath in horror. What the blazing fire had left the rains had finished. The result was a blackened mass, what was left of the canes beaten down into the muddy ground.

'Oh, Rod, it's awful! I'm sorry!' She didn't know how to express her sympathy or offer comfort. He turned without acknowledging her tremulous words and began the descent to the cottages. Here fresh evidence of last night's disaster awaited them. Rain had come through one section of the office as Rod had forseen and files and papers which had been left on the desk were saturated. There were puddles of rainwater on the floor. The whole place reeked of damp in the steamy heat.

'If you could help me to move the desk into the window recess so that the sun can reach it,' Lena suggested, 'I could spread the papers out to dry.' Even so, she knew, many of the documents and account statements would have to be retyped.

She saw Rod grit his teeth as he took the main weight of the desk on his wounded hands. She wished she hadn't asked him to help her. She could with an effort have pushed the desk across the floor on her own, she reproached herself.

Grimly silent, he left her to her task and went next door. After a few minutes he returned to gaze at her with a mixture of despair and defiance.

'The rain has come in next door too,' he announced. 'The mattress on my bed is soaked, so are the sheets and the covers. I wonder if you could help me to get them out into the sun to dry?'

She went with him eagerly. 'Oh, Rod,' she exclaimed when she saw how the rain had penetrated, 'this is terrible!'

'It wasn't normal rain,' Rod said doggedly. 'This has never happened before and with luck will never happen again.'

'But supposing it does? You really can't go on sleeping down here!'

He swung round on her with an exasperated air. 'Will you kindly mind your own business! I know you mean well, but this has nothing whatever to do with you. I'll get this room dried out by nightfall and this is where I'm sleeping. I don't know if it's occurred to you, but there are times when a man prefers solitude to a lot of female chatter. . . .'

'Mrs Clarens and I don't chatter,' Lena began resentfully, then broke off. This was no time to start a quarrel with poor Rod. He was tired, dispirited. The loss of the sugar cane had hit him hard—as though it were in fact his own property. Did he in some instinctive way difficult to control feel that indeed it was?

They were dragging the mattress out into the little forecourt, the sun like a palpable weight on their bare heads and shoulders.

'What about Mandy's room?' Lena asked.

'I haven't looked yet.'

When they did look they found that it had fared better than the office and Rod's room, but it seemed very damp and steamy. 'It isn't a fit place for her to sleep. . . .' Lena couldn't keep the words back.

Rod shrugged in a defeated way. 'Well, if you and

Mrs Clarens have made up your minds that she'd better remain up at the house I suppose that's the way it has to be.'

It was a grudging concession. But in his present mood Lena felt she could hardly expect any more.

It was as she followed him out of the cottage, passing through his bedroom on the way, that she saw the coloured photograph of Dolores on the table by his bed, a replica of the picture kept in the lounge at Windara House. There was a little vase of fresh flowers placed before it . . . as though it were a shrine. Wattle and daisy weed, the sort of bouquet a child would put together.

Mandy was delighted when she heard she was to continue sleeping at the big house. 'Why is it right for me to do it now when it wasn't right before?' she demanded, as they ate their rather makeshift lunch, Mrs Clarens' day having been thoroughly disorganised by events.

'Why?' Mandy persisted, when nobody answered her.

'Ask no questions and you'll be told no lies,' Mrs Clarens declared darkly.

Mandy fixed her big blue eyes on her father. 'You said it wouldn't be proper,' she reminded him. 'How did it get to be proper now?'

'Eat your pudding and don't chatter so much,' Mrs Clarens tried again repressively.

But it was no use. Mandy was still gazing expectantly at her father, who invariably took her questions seriously.

'I thought Lena might like to have the house to herself when she first came as she didn't know us very well,' he improvised.

'And now she knows us it's all right,' Mandy nodded. And after a moment: 'But why aren't you going to come and sleep up here too?'

'I prefer to sleep down at the cottage so as to be near the office,' he offered a little uncertainly. But the explanation served to silence the little girl, though she continued to look puzzled.

'You're going to have the little room next to mine,' Mrs Clarens told her.

Mandy pondered this a moment and then, brightening, said, 'Couldn't I sleep in Lena's room? It's very big and there would be lots of room for me.'

Nobody answered this unexpected request for a moment. Would Mrs Clarens be offended at this hint of favouritism for the newcomer? Lena wondered.

'Maybe Lena wouldn't want you in her room,' Rod suggested.

'Oh, yes, I'd love to have her,' Lena found herself saying a little too quickly.

'Goody!' Mandy exulted, and running round the table gave Lena an impulsive hug. 'You can tell me stories after I'm in bed. And we could play Ludo.'

'Into the small hours of the morning,' Rod laughed. It was the first time he had laughed since he had come in from the fire-fighting. Was he pleased at the new sleeping arrangement? Lena wondered, and met his swift, vital glance.

'You will undress me and put me to bed, won't you?' Leaning close to Lena, Mandy gazed up at her anxiously.

'Yes, I'll put you to bed,' Lena promised, moved by the little girl's advances, conscious of the weight of the small warm body against her own. Tenderness stirred in her as she drew the child closer.

'That's settled, then.' Rod stood up. 'And now

come along, Mandy, and I'll get you off to school. No need for you to miss a whole day.'

'It wouldn't do her any harm,' Mrs Clarens muttered. 'How are you going to manage the wheel of the launch with those blistered hands?' she asked Rod.

'We'll be running with the tide,' Rod reminded her, 'and on the way back I'll call in on the doctor and have the benefit of professional dressings for my hands. Besides, I must get my suit to the cleaners and I'd like a shampoo to get rid of some of this soot and smoke in my hair.'

'Oh, well, if that's how it is. . . .' Mrs Clarens began gathering up the used plates.

'Are you sure you don't mind having Mandy in your room?' Rod asked Lena. For the moment they were alone at the end of the two-purpose kitchen, Mandy having gone upstairs to fetch her school satchel, while Mrs Clarens clattered plates at the distant sink.

'Don't let her bulldoze you into it!'

'Oh, she's not bulldozing me,' Lena returned quickly. 'I shall love having her with me.'

Rod gave her an uneasy glance. 'As long as she doesn't become too attached to you. You're not exactly a permanency in her life, are you?'

Lena felt her heart shrink. Was there any need for him to have reminded her how transient her effect on their lives must be? 'Children take things and people as they come,' she offered.

'And as they go,' he added. Was he trying to hurt her? But of course he wasn't. It wouldn't occur to him how painful the thought of her return to England was becoming . . . especially after the events of last night. The tragic fire seemed to have drawn her more deeply into the life at Windara with all its beauty and hazards.

Later she went with Mrs Clarens to the cottage to move some of Mandy's things. There were several dolls and a large ancient teddy bear to be retrieved, besides the little girl's modest collection of clothes.

'Ridiculous putting her down here in the first place,' Mrs Clarens grumbled, looking around the dark, damp room. 'But Rod has been that obstinate since Tom Shannon died. That stupid will has cut him to the heart.' She shook her head. 'Why couldn't the old man have divided the property, or at least the value of it, between the three of you—you and Rod and that New Zealand cousin. Rod could have stayed on here then and worked the place, sending you and the cousin your share of the profits. In that way Tom wouldn't have upset your life, dragging you all the way out here at an old man's whim.'

So that was how it seemed to Mrs Clarens and no doubt to Rod. They were right, of course; you couldn't order two people to fall in love and get married in order to accommodate the upkeep of an estate. Unless, of course, they got married without falling in love. This unexpected notion lingered in Lena's mind a moment and then was firmly dismissed. There was no way out of the dilemma for her but to return to England in due course. The only advantage in prolonging her stay at Windara was that it enabled Rod . . . and herself, of course . . . to continue to receive the monthly portions of the six months' payment.

But there were times when the difficulties of life at Windara outweighed the financial advantages. Last night, for instance, when she waited for Rod to return from that raging inferno on the hillside. The thought of his danger even now made her feel sick and weak —as if it had been a part of her own self up there on the hill exposed to the fury of the flames. In a way, she realised with a pang, it *had* been a part of herself, the part that all unbidden she had given to this enigmatic Australian stranger. She felt her nerves tingle, as if he were there beside her, touching her, looking at her with his inscrutable gaze.

Clutching the big teddy bear to her breast, she went out on to the shabby verandah where Mrs Clarens was pronouncing Rod's sunbaked mattress to be 'bone dry'.

'Let's carry it indoors and make up the poor lad's bed,' she suggested. 'He will only allow me to clean down here once a week. Proper old hermit he's turning into! Moody, that's what he is. Ever since you came . . . or rather ever since that crazy will was sprung on him.'

Heavy of heart, Lena could think of no suitable comment.

Later, it was Rod who moved Mandy's bed into her room. He seemed a bit more cheerful and was looking spruce after his shampoo and trim, the burned-blond hair now regaining some of its lustre. The doctor had given him some tablets to ease his various aches and pains and had applied a bandage to the strained ankle. 'Now,' he exulted, as he spoke of these remedies to Lena, 'I'll be able to tackle the shambles up on the hill!'

'Do you think you can salvage any of the sugar cane?' Lena asked, as they tucked sheets into the made-up bed in companionable fashion.

'We shall see when it dries out,' he told her. 'The burned canes are finished, of course, but where they were only waterlogged they'll probably pick up. This is a wonderfully accommodating climate in spite of the odd catastrophe.'

Mandy came running in with her teddy bear in her

arms. 'Oh, goody!' she cried when she saw the newly made bed. 'Teddy must go to bed at once. He's tired out after his long walk up from the cottage,' she explained as she tucked him firmly between the sheets.

Rod and Lena stood side by side, looking down at her. She was at this moment so like the girl in the coloured photograph that it was quite uncanny—a miniature Dolores, mothering her toy, her every movement curiously full of grace. She would dance as naturally as she breathed, Lena thought, and heard her say that there was going to be a dancing display at the school in Latonga next week. 'All the children's mummies and daddies are coming,' she told Rod. 'Will you come, Daddy?'

'Of course I will.' Lena didn't miss the flash of pain across his mobile face. Just a daddy this time. No mummy.

Mandy, as if sensing the omission, glanced from her father to Lena with an odd wistfulness. 'Lena could come too,' she said, and added cryptically, 'All the other children will have two people. . . .'

'I'd love to come,' Lena assured the little girl, making her tone light and matter-of-fact. She saw Rod turn away to stand by the dressing table, gazing blindly at its array of cosmetics. With a fingertip he touched the drooping jacaranda blossoms in their glass of water. 'You've been rifling your tree,' he said. 'But the jacaranda flowers don't last long, either indoors or out. Spring flowers which bloom before the leaves. Last night they took a battering in the rain storm, which will have shortened their time with us. We'll have to wait until next spring to see them again in all their glory.'

But neither of them would be here next spring . . . had he forgotten? And why did he speak now of jacaranda blossoms?

'Beauty whose hand is ever at its lips
Bidding farewell . . .' Lena whispered.

His startled glance held . . . was it a question? . . .
an appeal? It was not the passing beauty of a springtime tree he mourned but the lost springtime of his own
youth.

I should have left Keats and the haunting quality of
his poetry alone, Lena thought with remorse.

By the time Sunday came round Rod declared himself
ready for a day on the surfing beach. They had made
better progress than he could have hoped with the
salvage work in the cane fields and his dark mood
seemed to have lifted. It was amazing to Lena how
soon the rains drained away and the ground dried up.
The river too had shrunk to its normal dimensions, so
that the daily journeyings to Latonga with Mandy were
resumed.

'How about it?' Rod challenged Lena across the
breakfast table. 'Would you like to come and have a
shot at surfing? I can hire a board for you.'

'Can I come too?' Mandy put in before Lena had
time to reply.

'Of course you can, poppet,' Rod was quick to as-
sure the little girl. 'We'll go to Doora Heads where
we'll be certain to find a bunch of your school pals,
complete with mums, who can keep an eye on you
while Lena and I challenge the Pacific breakers.'

'Do you think I dare?' Lena asked a trifle breathlessly.

'I'll see you don't completely drown,' he laughed.
And then more seriously, 'We'll go to the end of the
beach where the sea is comparatively manageable.'

'What is it going to do to your hands, putting them

into sea water?' Mrs Clarens asked Rod.

'Salt water is the best thing in the world for blistered hands. It has healing properties. Anyway, they're better now.' He held them out for inspection.

Mrs Clarens nodded, satisfied. Lena, aware of the older woman's motherly concern for the young man, felt a twinge of pity. What would she do, where would she go when the household broke up? For years Windara had been her home . . . she had watched over Rod, and Uncle Tom before him. Would she be able to stay on and look after the cousin from New Zealand? But it was possible that the unknown relative would sell the place, perhaps without even coming to see it. If only things could stay as they are now, Lena thought sadly.

But half an hour later on the way to Doora Heads in the comfortable Toyota she was filled with a sense of delightful expectancy which held no room for regrets. It was enough that the sun was shining out of a cloudless sky and the thrill of learning to surf with Rod lay before her.

'We'll stop off in the town and hire that surfing board for you,' Rod reminded her.

Lena gave an exaggerated shiver. 'I'm terrified,' she confessed. 'I shall never be able to keep upright in those boiling breakers!'

'You just have to take it easy,' Rod assured her. 'You can swim and you've done a little water-skiing, you tell me, so you should be able to control your board.'

'I'll choose nice little ones for you,' he joked. 'But big waves or lesser ones, the principle is the same. You have to adjust to the speed of the water—go along with it. It's a wonderful sensation, like flying, only even more exciting. The water seems to have a life

108

of its own. You have to become one with it.'

His lean face glowed as he spoke. For once he seemed as young as his twenty-seven years. For a brief moment he was carefree, the burned-out cane fields forgotten. Perhaps even the loss of Dolores was receding, fading as it ultimately should into the past where it belonged. He was too young to spend the rest of his life mourning. Meanwhile the golden day caressed them. If they could seize on it . . . make the most of it; let both the past and the future troubles be forgotten.

Walking down the gay little high street at Doora they lingered to look in shop windows. Mandy wanted an ice cream, so Rod took them into the garden of a smart hotel, where they sat beneath the shade of a rose pergola and drank chilled fruit juice. Brilliant flower beds were spread before them, scarlet poincianas, gardenias, hibiscus heavy with orange-gold blooms and flowers of dark red velvet. The perfume of frangipani filled the air.

'They do a marvellous evening meal here,' Rod announced. 'We must come over one evening.'

'Was it a dinner date he was offering her? Lena's spirit soared. No need now to push past and future aside. The present was enough, and today it was all sunshine, the light breeze from the sea with its tang of salt heady as champagne.

When the business of hiring the surfing board had been accomplished they made their way over a hilly sand-dune to the beach, already crowded with week-end sun-worshippers. As Rod had predicted, Latonga acquaintances were thick on the ground—literally, gay family groups sheltering under their vast coloured umbrellas. Mandy was left with a kindly Mrs Arnott, watching over her brood of seven lively youngsters.

'You have more courage than I have,' she said, eyeing Lena's surfing board.

Lena laughingly admitted that she had no courage at all for this her first attempt at surfing. But beneath her nervousness excitement tingled. In a moment she had slipped off her cotton dress and clad—or unclad—suitably in her bikini was going down the sloping beach with Rod, now stripped to his trunks. The fibreglass surfing board she carried was light and the sand gloriously warm and soft beneath her feet. As they approached the water Rod took her hand, his fingers closing firmly over her own.

'No shivering on the brink,' he warned her. 'We plunge in and let the water take us.' He showed her how to place her feet on the surfing board, letting her find her balance in the shallows. Then suddenly, as they waded in, a great wave crashed down upon them and Lena found herself being carried away. Just for one dizzy moment she managed to hold on to her stance on the board and felt herself riding on the crest of a foam-topped slope, looking down into a valley of jade-green water. Then the impetus of the wave flung her down into the valley and she lost her board. Terrifyingly she was submerged, fighting her way through the boiling foam, the power of the great ocean having its way with her. Utterly helpless, she gasped and struggled, until somehow Rod was beside her, his own surfing board abandoned. She felt his hands beneath her arms, dragging her clear of the torrent of water. Slipping on the sliding sands, she managed to get to her feet, her wet hair streaming about her shoulders. Rod kept his arm about her until they reached the safety of the firm sand above the tide line.

Dashing the water out of her eyes, she laughed up at him. 'It was marvellous!' she said breathlessly, forgetting the moments of panic and helplessness, remembering only that he had come to her aid.

'You did very well,' he commended her. 'Like to have another go?' Without waiting for her answer he ran along the shore to retrieve their surfing boards.

By the end of the morning she was able to keep upright for minutes at a time and if ultimately there was the inevitable crash into the breakers it was all part of the fun. So was lying on the beach afterwards drying out in the hot sunshine. Stretched out on his towel at her side, Rod leaned up on his elbow to look down at her. The silence between them was drowsy and peaceful, born of the utter physical well-being which comes after strenuous exercise in the sea. Glancing away at the group of surfers in the rougher water further down the beach, Rod said, 'Pete will be mad he missed out on your surfing initiation. He had to go to Sydney on some kind of car business this weekend.'

Lena offered no comment.

'He could have done his gallant-knight-to-the-rescue act again,' Rod needled her.

Lena laughed, 'One gallant knight at a time is quite enough, and as it happens my preference is for the one who helped me today.'

Rod sat up abruptly. 'What about those sandwiches Mrs Clarens prepared for us?' he said.

Later when they had collected Mandy and given her her share of the sandwiches and fruit they walked round the inlet of water, sheltered by the twin headlands which gave the district its name. Climbing to the highest point above the trees and shrubs, they stood looking out at the expanse of sea and sky spread before them. The Pacific, stretching to the farthest horizon, was a restless wilderness of blue and jade-green water, tossed by 'white horses'.

111

'Pacific is surely the wrong name for it,' Lena murmured half to herself. 'It looks so powerful, so uncontrollable.'

'You should see it when it's really rough,' Rod told her. 'When, for instance, we get the odd hurricane. Then the wind comes roaring inland with the full rage of the sea behind it. Trees, rooftops, cars . . . anything that gets in the path of the hurricane is hurled into space.'

Mandy, who had vanished for a few minutes, appeared, a small tabby cat in her wake. 'It's lost, Daddy.' The little girl was half tearful. 'I know it's lost. It came up to me crying. . . .'

'People, if you can call them people,' Rod spat the words out in utter contempt, 'bring their unwanted pets up here into the wilds and abandon them.'

Mandy had the kitten in her arms by now. It was pitifully thin, its golden eyes watching Rod's face eagerly, as if it knew its fate rested with him.

'May I take it home?' Mandy begged. The kitten-cat was kneading her shoulder now, purring loudly as if it had no doubt as to what the answer to the little girl's question would be.

'I suppose we'll have to take it,' Rod conceded. 'We can't leave it here to starve to death. I wish one could find the inhuman monsters who do this kind of thing to animals.' His tone held cold fury.

They went back to the beach to collect their things, the kitten determinedly following them. There was some milk left in Mandy's luncheon thermos, which it drank ravenously and even ate part of a ham sandwich.

Going home in the comfortable Toyota it curled itself up on Mandy's not very ample lap and purred itself to sleep.

'What shall we call it?' Mandy asked.

'Puss-puss,' Rod suggested, without much originality.

'Tiger,' Lena tried. 'It's got such lovely stripey markings.'

'It wouldn't be very nice to call it Tiger if it's a girl,' Mandy pointed out. 'Even if it's a boy it's much too fierce a name.'

'Call it Goldie, then,' said Lena. 'Because it has such lovely golden eyes, and we found it on such a lovely golden day.' She met Rod's quick oddly sensitive glance over the little girl's head.

'Goldie!' Mandy exulted. 'That's exackerly right. Goldie!' she crooned, and picking the kitten up limp with sleep she buried her lips in its soft fur. 'We'll keep it all our lives, won't we?' she demanded anxiously of her father.

'It won't live as long as we will, I'm afraid,' he pointed out. 'But we'll see it's all right as long as we can,' he added doubtfully.

Was he thinking of the time when they must all leave Windara? Lena wondered. Where would they go . . . Rod and his little daughter . . . and the lost kitten? Up to now she had instinctively avoided facing up to this question, but now it struck her with all its poignancy. Earlier she had worried over Mrs Clarens' prospects, but now it was the fate of Rod and Mandy which haunted her. Three people to be made homeless . . . all because of the intransigence of an old man's will. Or perhaps because in his bachelor innocence he had assumed too much. Two people falling in love because of the material benefit they would get out of it. Ironically, he had given them six months in which to achieve this miracle of compatability. But Rod's indifference and indeed mistrust towards her seemed to increase with every day that passed. Today for the first time he had relaxed his guard, become approachable. But

113

the guard was still there. Apart altogether from the strange conditions of Uncle Tom's it was difficult to imagine Rod ever falling in love with her, Lena thought sadly.

The light was dying out of the sky now with the rapidly increasing twilight, even as the light of this one happy day died out of her heart. So that she was wholly taken by surprise when, as they approached the house, Rod turned to her and said, ' How would you feel about turning right round and going back to Doora Heads after you've had a wash and changed? Tonight would be as good a night as any for that dinner at the Pearl Beach Hotel.'

She couldn't answer him for a moment, then she stammered her acceptance of his invitation.

' Don't come unless you really want to,' he said, mis-understanding her hesitation.

' But I do want to,' she told him with an eagerness which shamed her. Then throwing caution to the winds, she added, ' There's nothing I would like better in the whole world!'

He nodded. ' Me too,' he murmured so softly, that she couldn't be quite sure he had really said it.

CHAPTER VII

It was a good hour before they were back on the road again. Apart from the business of changing there had been Mandy to put to bed. Since sleeping in Lena's room she had insisted that it was Lena herself who should superintend the evening ritual. Then there was the problem of Goldie. Mrs Clarens had accepted the little cat with a minimum of fuss, but drew the line at Goldie being allowed to sleep on Mandy's bed.

'The kitten must sleep in the conservatory porch,' Mrs Clarens decreed. 'I'll give her an earth pan and see that she's safely shut in. Not that she would run away after all that chicken and milk. Lost cats know when they're well off.' And even before Mandy went up to bed the little stray had settled down for the night in a comfortable shawl-filled basket.

'I'll go to sleep quickly,' Mandy had said, as Lena kissed her good night. 'Then it will soon be morning and I can run downstairs and let Goldie out. She might be lonely waking up by herself.'

There was just time after that for a hurried shower. Opening her wardrobe, Lena wondered what she should wear. The backless white dress was a bit too elaborate perhaps for a simple dinner date. She chose a calf-length turquoise dress with a full skirt and chiffon sleeves. There was a string of turquoise beads to go with it, an old-fashioned necklace which had belonged to her mother.

'Are you and Daddy going to a party?' Mandy enquired from her bed drowsily.

'Just out to dinner,' Lena answered. But already the little girl was drifting off to sleep.

Rod, spruce in his freshly cleaned suit, was waiting on the verandah when Lena went downstairs.

'What it is to be young and have endless energy!' Mrs Clarens remarked enviously as she saw them off. But there was warmth and good will in her smile.

She's growing to like me, Lena thought, remembering with what obvious reservations the older woman had first received her. Now perhaps she was beginning to hope that things might turn out happily for them all in the end . . . if this dinner date was any kind of a good omen!

Darkness had fallen as the Toyota sped smoothly over the highway. The moon rose to swim in a cloudless sky. It was warm inside the car, the faint aroma of Lena's special perfume sweetening the air. Had she used it too generously? she wondered uneasily when Rod, rolling his window down, said they ought to have a little fresh air. He leaned across her to lower the window on her side of the car, and for a brief instant she felt the weight of his shoulder against her own. His crisp dark-gold hair brushed her cheek. She caught her breath, conscious of his nearness and of her own involuntary response to it in the perfumed darkness.

A moment later he was swinging the car into a layby, bringing it to a stop. Now what? Her heart beat unevenly. Rod wasn't the type to go in for casual petting sessions—or so she would have thought. But she needn't have worried.

'Come and have a look at our famous constellation, the Southern Cross,' he was saying as he got out of the car. The stars which are the emblem of Australia's national flag.

Hurrying round, he opened the door on Lena's side of the Toyota and helped her out. His hand-clasp was cool as he led her over the grass verge. The sky was a velvety expanse scintillating with stars so numerous and brilliant that the light of the moon could not dim them. Lena looked up at them, trying to distinguish the famous Cross.

'Look over towards the west,' Rod advised. With an arm about her shoulder he swung her round, holding her close to him as together they found the constellation.

'It takes a bit of imagination to see it as a cross,' was Lena's rather breathless comment. Stars and moonlight and Rod. Her senses swam.

Releasing her, he laughed. 'Don't be so literal. Five mystical stars, isn't that enough for you, even if the cross isn't entirely symmetrical?'

Back in the car, on their way again, they spoke little. But it was a companionable silence.

All too soon they were cruising down the high street of the little coastal town. When they had parked the car Rod asked, 'How would your shoes stand up to a short walk on the beach? You ought to see the Pacific by moonlight.'

They climbed the steep sand dune which backed on the parking place and there was the great stretch of moonlit ocean before them, the breakers sparkling white as they crashed shorewards. They stood side by side, Lena lost in the magic of the scene, her feverish thoughts stilled. Even her awareness of Rod didn't disturb her now. Self-concern vanished and with it self-consciousness. In the face of that immensity of sea and starlit sky she felt that for a moment she was part of something much greater than herself and her own small worries. Time ceased to exist. It was with a start that she heard Rod say, 'Magnificent, isn't it? But perhaps we'd better go and eat.'

A sudden descent to the mundane which banished

her mystical mood. With a sigh she turned away from the swaying, crashing tide, stumbling a little in the loose sand as they made their way to the high street.

The restaurant at the Pearl Beach Hotel was small and intimate, the light pleasantly muted. There were candle-shaped lamps under rosy shades on the tables and shallow dishes of pink and white lotus flowers.

'Drinks first,' Rod began. 'What will you have? Vermouth? Martini?'

'Martini—dry,' Lena chose. She touched one of the candlelamps with a fingertip. 'A flattering light,' she murmured.

'You don't need the flattery of a muted light,' Rod returned with what might have been the automatic gallantry the occasion demanded. Only that there was nothing automatic about the intense way he was looking at her. It brought back her self-consciousness.

'Thanks,' she said, 'but I wish I'd had time to do something about my hair.' She put a tentative hand to it. 'It's full of salt water after my tussle with the breakers this morning.'

'Is that why you bundled it up on top of your head?' he enquired.

She laughed. 'Bundled up, indeed! If you knew the trouble I went to in order to fix it the way it is!'

'I like it,' he told her. 'Though it's nice too when you wear it down, loose. This way it makes you look more grown up.'

'I *am* grown up,' she said. 'All of twenty-two years to my credit, and during three of those I've lived in London on my own.'

'On your own?' he echoed doubtfully.

'Well, I shared a flat with two other girls, but to all practical intents and purposes I was managing my own affairs.'

'What about boy-friends?' There was veiled laughter in his glance.

'Inquisitive, aren't you?' she objected.

He shrugged. 'I was just wondering. . . . Have you ever been in love?'

'Yes,' she answered shortly. I'm in love right now, she could have added.

'Yes,' he mimicked her monosyllable. 'Full stop. I've no right to be probing, have I?'

Her eyes were wide with distress as she looked at him across the candlelit table. Words would not come. What words *could* there be?

'It didn't go well,' he hazarded. 'Too bad. Poor Lena!' Lightly he dismissed her girlish distresses. The wine waiter had brought the drinks. Rod raised his glance. 'Here's to better luck next time. The world,' he added carelessly, 'is full of Pete Fosters.'

'Do you mind if we change the subject?' Her tone was frigid. She had had about as much as she could stand of this snide quizzing and was relieved when a second waiter appeared at her side, placing an outsize menu card before her.

'Seafood is a speciality here,' Rod advised. 'What about starting with one of their prawn cocktails?'

They went on from that to lobster Mornay. Lena found she was ravenously hungry. It was a good many hours since they had had those sandwiches on the beach.

'I could still eat a horse,' Rod confessed, when the lobster had been disposed of. They ordered chicken au cognac with succulent petits pois and glazed baby carrots, ending the meal with a mouthwatering pineapple soufflé.

Over coffee and liqueurs they sat somnolent and at peace.

'This is nice,' Rod sighed with satisfaction as he lit a cigar. 'A delicious meal . . . a charming companion.'

Lena wished he hadn't added the final stereotyped gallantry. 'This is nice,' spoken with feeling, would have been enough.

'You don't hate me, then?' she blurted, and instantly regretted her impulsiveness. But it was too late to withdraw the foolish question. Rod had started forward. placing his elbows on the table, leaning towards her. In the candlelight his sun-tanned face was taut.

'Hate you? What on earth are you getting at?'

If only she could have told him what this hour of intimate companionship meant to her! Had she been wrong in feeling he was enjoying it as much as she herself?

'Come on,' he insisted. 'Why should I hate you?'

'Oh, I don't know!' She tried to shrug it off. 'I get the feeling at times that I'm all wrong at Windara. That I ought never to have come.'

'It would have meant the early end of Windara for Mandy and me if you hadn't. At least as things are I've got time to work out what I must do when the inevitable finale overtakes us.'

It wasn't the answer she would have hoped for. 'What do you think you *will* do?' she ventured.

'I honestly don't know,' Rod confessed, passing a distracted hand through his thick hair. In the gentle light there were golden glints in it. The glance fixed on her was full of questions, uncertainties. He looked at that moment young and lost.

'I could go back to my old job, I suppose. But it would mean living in a big town—not so good for Mandy. However, I shall soon have to be putting out feelers.'

There was desolation in his tone; the contentment

which bound them together a few moments before was utterly shattered. What on earth had possessed her to wreck the mood with her silly question about being hated? Lena wondered savagely. Rod and Mandy caught in the turmoil of a city. Mrs Clarens looking for another job as housekeeper in a world where grey hairs are not an asset. Suddenly Lena could see it all. A wave of despair swept over her. It must not be allowed to happen. Somehow she must prevent it . . . and there was only one way. She took a deep swallow of the liqueur in her glass. 'Why can't things go on at Windara as they are?' she suggested, her voice not quite steady.

'How do you mean?' Rod's tone was sharp. 'Six months is our limit.'

Lena took another drink and drew a long breath. 'Unless we marry,' she reminded him.

Rod's look was one of utter astonishment. 'Marry?' he echoed blankly.

In spite of the liqueur, Lena's mouth was so dry she could hardly go on. 'There are such things as marriages of convenience,' she reminded him. 'A marriage in name only . . . to cover certain circumstances. Such an arrangement would save you from having to leave Windara to look for other work . . . another home. And there's Mrs Clarens,' she added hurriedly in the electrical silence which followed her proposal. 'I know she's dreading the upheaval . . .' the words trailed away.

'And what about your own angle on this extraordinary proposition?' Rod asked with biting scorn. 'You haven't mentioned how much it would do for you. A solid background for keeps, a comfortable home instead of a bed-sitter shared with two other girls, property to your name, money in the bank, an assured future . . .

and a mock marriage thrown in for good measure.' His burst of laughter hit her like a whiplash. ' The things people will do for money! But somehow I didn't think of you as a cold-blooded fortune-hunter. But I suppose with a broken romance on your hands this seems as good a way out as any other.'

Waves of misery washed over her as she listened to this outburst. But what, in heaven's name, had she expected? She must have been out of her mind to imagine she could so easily settle Rod's problems. The happy atmosphere of the evening had betrayed her, and she knew now that she had been hoping against hope and that it wasn't a mock marriage she had really been suggesting. Throughout the long golden day she had sensed a unity with Rod Carron. The barriers of misunderstanding and mistrust seemed to have vanished. In his glances, in his touch, in things he had said and left unsaid there had been significant indications. Or so she had instinctively felt. But she had been wrong, tragically wrong. Her ' instinct' had been wholly unfounded, imaginary.

' It was just . . . a wild idea,' she offered weakly.

Rod knocked the ash off his cigar with a savage gesture. ' I wish I could believe you. But I suppose it's natural in your circumstances to want to cling to Windara, however clumsily you go about it.' He shrugged. ' Somehow I thought you would have been more fastidious. A marriage in name only,' he mocked. ' What sort of a man do you think I am? Can you imagine the kind of life we would lead? Each one of us knowing the other was merely in the contract for material gain. I'd rather starve!' His voice rose passionately and and the look he flashed at her in the candlelight was one of sheer dislike.

' Silly of me,' he went on, ' but one has one's illusions: I never suspected you were the kind of girl who would launch a proposition like this. And even so, if you'd hoped we might forget all the things that make a marriage worth while in order to cash in on a crazy old man's will, you might have waited for *me* to come up with the idea.'

Each word he spoke was a blow over her heart. Rod seeing her as someone cheap, grasping, utterly insensitive—a barefaced fortune-hunter, brazenly offering herself in a sordid bargain. Why had she plunged in so unthinkingly? But it wasn't only the happiness of this day which led her on, it was the growing awareness of the problems confronting Rod. He had worked for Windara for years. He loved every acre of the fruitful land, fighting the fire that awful night practically with his bare hands. How could he leave it all now? But he would never believe her desire to help him was the main driving force in her ill-considered plan for a marriage of convenience.

She picked up her handbag and said with what dignity she could muster, 'I seem to have put my foot in it completely. I suppose it's too much to hope that you might give me the benefit of the doubt . . . try to believe me when I tell you that it was your side of all this I was thinking of. You and Mandy.'

His burst of laughter was like a slap in the face. Her lips quivered. 'How can I stay on at Windara now that you feel I'm nothing more than a clumsy fortune-hunter? Perhaps I ought to go back to England straight away.'

'That's right,' he nodded sardonically. 'Cut and run now that you've found there isn't really any future at Windara for you. Abandon what's left of our six months of stability. What about all the touching concern you are supposed to have for me and for Mandy?

Aren't we even going to have time to find a new location before we're flung out into the world? And what about the cane fields and pineapple plantations? What's going to happen to the salvaging if I'm forced to leave the property at this critical time? Honestly, Lena! Will you try to think of someone beside yourself for a moment?'

She pressed her evening bag against her breast, as if to ease the pain there. 'It wasn't that way, Rod, really it wasn't. I was not thinking of myself in what I suggested. You don't know the first thing about me. If you did. . . .' Her voice broke, she couldn't go on. Tears shone on her lashes.

'Come on!' he said roughly. 'Let's get out of here before we have a weeping session.' Leaving a reckless pile of dollar bills on the table, he took her arm and guided her hurriedly from the room.

'I'm sorry if I was a bit brutal with you just now,' he offered in a grudging tone as they left the hotel. 'Let's forget it. Blame it all on Uncle Tom and his lack of understanding. Didn't he realise that even if we had obliged him by falling in love it couldn't have worked out? A marriage based on financial gain would be a breeding ground for suspicion—worse even than your ghastly notion of a marriage of convenience. The more I loved you the more impossible it would be for me. In every way my position would be invidious. Because it's you who bear the name of Shannon, you who are the relative, the true heiress to the Shannon wealth. If I was brought into it it was because you couldn't have run the place on your own. It was vital that you should have my experience to help you. And the old man was fond of me. All this would poison our relationship at every turn, destroying all trust.' Did she imagine the regret in his tone? They were out of the hotel garden now, walking down the brightly lit street with its gay little shops and flowering trees.

'I'm sorry, Rod,' she managed. 'I didn't think of it like that. In fact I didn't think it all out at all . . . it was just that I can't imagine Windara without you. Please believe me.'

He laughed. 'I'll try. And you're not booking that London flight from Brisbane in the morning?'

'No,' she said, 'I'm not doing that. I'll stand by you as long as you need me.'

'As long as I'm allowed by the contents of that damned will to need you. And don't forget, you're getting something out of it too—a nice fat allowance for the rest of our strange six months.'

'I won't forget, Rod.' She was too dispirited to defend herself any more.

And soon they were on their way back to Windara, the organ note of the Pacific surf dying away behind them. The golden day with its promise was over. If only it had not been such a happy day! I never want to go surfing again as long as I live, Lena thought. There was a taste of dust and ashes in her mouth, and the pain in her heart was sharper than she could bear. All she wanted now was the solitude of her room, a long dark night in which she could fight her way out of her black mood of despair.

During the week which followed she saw little of Rod. Still engrossed with the salvaging of the fruit crops, he was out and about at first light and worked in the fields all day, taking sandwiches with him for lunch. When he appeared for the evening meal he ate mostly in silence, leaving the house as soon as he could afterwards, not even waiting to spend a little time with Mandy in his usual way. He had things to do at the cottage, he would excuse himself.

'Proper out of sorts, he is,' Mrs Clarens commented one evening when he had taken himself off with even less explanation than usual. 'It's the fire damage getting him down. He seemed to be standing up to it at first, but this last week he's lost all his spirit. I've never known him so depressed.' The old lady sighed. 'I suppose it's natural enough. He loves Windara as if it were his own. All the years he's lived for it and worked for it . . . it will break his heart when he has to leave it to the mercy of a stranger.'

She glanced at Lena over her spectacles—she was busy darning a pair of Rod's white knee-length socks —'I suppose,' she mused, 'there's no chance of the two of you being able to fit in with Tom Shannon's strange will?'

'Not a chance in the world,' Lena answered shortly, and standing up said she had better go and see if Mandy had settled down to sleep. The prospect of discussing her uncle's will with Mrs Clarens filled her with horror. It would be intolerable to have to endure the old lady's probing questions as she searched for some gleam of hope in the situation which was so rapidly closing in on them all.

Sunday came and went and there was no suggestion from Rod of a surfing trip. Lena went to church with Mrs Clarens and Mandy and later took the little girl riding—to the obvious delight of Billy-Boy and Melody —two more inhabitants of Windara whose future was uncertain, Lena thought sadly.

But everything that happened now seemed to her eloquent of impermanence. And the days went by so quickly. Looking round the house she would catch herself thinking of the changes she could have made if she had been planning to live here permanently. The rooms were large and attractively designed, but the whole place needed freshening up, redecorating. The curtains and carpets were worn and shabby, the furniture mixed; some of it genuinely beautiful antiques, the rest a hotch-potch of ancient and modern chosen without discrimination, comfortable but ugly. A home that had belonged to a lonely bachelor—needing a woman's touch.

The cliché suggested itself to Lena with an echo of melancholy. Would there ever be a woman who would rejoice in bringing the place to life, making it as beautiful as it could be? Did the New Zealander cousin have a wife? she wondered. If only she herself had a free hand. But such thoughts were futile . . . and unbearably painful. It was as though in some remote corner of her heart she felt she had a right to this old family home, just as Rod felt he had a right over the cane fields and fruit plantations.

It was during that week which followed that Mandy reminded Lena that it was the day for the dancing display at her school. 'I told Daddy when he was saying goodnight to me last night,' the little girl went on. 'And he says he won't forget to come to it.'

Lena wondered if, in his present mood, he would ask her to accompany him. It was so clear that he had been avoiding her since the night of their dinner date when with a clumsiness at which she could now only wonder she had spoken of a marriage of convenience between them. He even managed his share of the office work with a minimum of contact, checking up on the documents she had had to retype after the fire and the rain.

On the day of the dancing display she took Mandy to morning school as usual. When she returned to the house it was to find that the mail had arrived and with it a further instalment of the generous monthly allowance Mr McKindry was paying her out of her uncle's estate. There was a similar letter containing a cheque for Rod.

'Perhaps you would pay it into the bank for me when you deposit your own cheque,' he suggested to Lena. He had appeared at lunch time for once and spoke now of the dancing display, taking it as accepted that Lena would be accompanying him.

'Mandy would be disappointed if you didn't show up,' he qualified his invitation. His mouth was grimly set, his eyes dark with their secret sorrow. Dancing, Lena thought. Dolores. The two would be inextricably mixed in his mind . . . his heart. If only Dolores were here today to see her small daughter's performance!

'Be ready about two,' he instructed Lena. 'Meet me down at the landing stage. I'm going along to the cottage now to change—can't turn up at the school in my working togs.'

'It's too hot for a lounge suit,' Lena ventured.

'Too right, it is,' he agreed. 'I'll settle for a pair of my white shorts and a clean shirt to match . . . as long as you won't be ashamed to be seen with me so unconventionally dressed.'

He was actually smiling at her. Her heart lifted. 'It's not unconventional. White shorts and shirt are the invariable uniform for the well dressed man in Queensland, I notice, and very sensible too in the heat. Even Mr Bexley at the bank wears shirt and shorts and those snow-white socks.'

'Bexley,' Rod mused. 'Our chief accountant with the razor-sharp mind. I wonder what he makes of it all—you turning up periodically with these hefty cheques.'

'Oh, he takes it in his stride,' Lena declared. 'No
128

doubt he assumes—and rightly—that this money is part of whatever legacy Uncle Tom left to me . . . and separately, to you. It was natural enough for him to leave you something after your long years of service to him.'

'I suppose so,' Rod agreed a little doubtfully. 'Thank goodness Mrs Clarens can keep her mouth shut and that the locals have no idea of the crazy will poor old Tom wished on us. It would have provided them with gossip for months.'

Lena offered no comment. Uncle Tom's will was too dangerous a topic to enlarge upon, and anyhow it was time she was making herself ready for the trip to Latonga. Taking a shower, she found herself foolishly elated at the prospect of the run down the river with Rod. It was such a beautiful river, wild and wide, cutting through the bushland imperiously. Every day she grew to love it more and more.

The sun was blazing as they set off. The hottest hour of the afternoon and for once there wasn't a cooling breeze from the water. Even the cranes and ibises were too lazy to fish and the black swans dozed in the shallows. Lena sat in the prow of the launch getting all the air she could, while Rod guided the little craft over the rather swollen tide. There had been frequent showers during the past week interspersed with the hours of excessive heat—a typical weather condition for late spring in Queensland, Lena had gathered. But at least the rain kept the bush fires at bay.

When they reached the Latonga landing stage Rod helped her ashore, holding her hand a moment longer than was absolutely necessary. Their glances met, Rod's imperious, Lena's questioning. In that moment time halted and there was a throbbing awareness between them. Lena could feel it—clearer than speech and far more disturbing than words could have been. Then they were walking along the rough narrow path which led to the high street, inevitably so close to one another that at moments their shoulders touched. The sense of awareness increased, became a sense of harmony. But when they reached the wider pavements of the high street the brief illusion vanished, for it could only have been illusion, Lena told herself sadly. Rod was his distant, preoccupied self again.

The display was held in a central civic hall, the large auditorium buzzing with excited mums and children, with a sprinkling of fathers standing awkwardly around. Mandy rushed forward to greet Rod and Lena, a miniature ballerina in her brief frilly tutu and modification of blocked ballet slippers. She was too young yet for the real thing, her small feet unformed.

'This is my daddy,' she announced proudly to a small girl who had followed her.

'And your mummy?' enquired the child, smiling at Lena.

Mandy paused a moment before answering hesitantly. 'She isn't exackerly my mummy, but she puts me to bed and I sleep in her room. Sometimes she takes me into bed with her in the early morning.'

The small friend nodded understandingly. 'It's nice,' she said, 'when you get into bed with your mummy and daddy. I often do.'

Lena and Rod exchanged startled glances, then Rod grinned wickedly. Lena went crimson and was furious with herself.

The display got under way with a good deal of fussing about of teachers and small performers, but once it had started it was a charming sight. The children had been well taught and were not stiff in their movements. Whoever was responsible had been careful to guard their natural spontaneity. The girls were the most successful dancers, the small boys lumbering conscientiously after them.

Perhaps she was imagining it. Lena thought, but Mandy seemed to stand out from all the other small performers, moving with a fluid natural grace. Once or twice Lena cast a sidelong glance at the man sitting beside her. His face was set and grim. Was it Dolores' ghost dancing there before him? And would he be proud if Mandy made a career of ballet? Lena had ceased to be surprised at the interest shown in the art locally. Australia, she had discovered, was very ballet-conscious, from Sydney, visited by all the major ballet companies in the world, to Brisbane which ran its own excellent amateur ballet company. 'We're not all Outback hicks, you know,' Mrs Clarens had remarked dryly one day when Lena had expressed surprise at the interest Mandy's school took in dancing.

Tea followed the dancing and Lena found herself surrounded by the 'mums' she knew from her daily journeyings to the school. Most of them also knew Rod. If their glances at the couple tended to be slightly curious they were very tactful, accepting Lena's friendship with the young man. After all, they were living on the same estate, both connected in their different ways with the late Tom Shannon. And Lena's devotion to Mandy had made a lot of difference to the motherless little girl. Could it be that it might become permanent? The unspoken questions hung in the air.

By the time they left the hall the shadows were lengthening. Lena still found it difficult to get used to the brief early dusk, the sudden fall of darkness after sunset. When they reached the river the whole sky and the stretch of water before them was a deep glowing crimson. It burned right across the sky, illuminating the landscape, a fiery grandeur throwing the thickly wooded banks into dark relief. As the launch pushed out from the bank Lena wished they might have been propelling themselves with oars. The chug-chug of the little craft's engine was an intrusion into the evening silence. Apparently Rod felt this too, for presently he cut out the engine and let the boat drift on the current for a while.

Mandy, tired after her excitement, snuggled into Lena's arms and fell asleep. They were passing near to the island now, with its legend of the tragic Caloola.

'Caloola Island.' Rod said. 'Do you remember Caloola? The beautiful girl who chose death rather than submit to an arranged marriage. If it were a little darker we might see her ghost, sitting on the white strand, combing her long hair and weeping for her lost lover.'

Why had he recalled the old legend? Was it a way of taunting her? Lena wondered with a stirring of indignation. Reminding her of that ghastly evening at the Pearl Beach hotel, and her clumsy suggestion of a marriage of convenience between them.

She said sharply, 'There would be more point to the story if Caloola had fished her wounded lover out of the river and nursed him back to health instead of drowning with him. But that would have spoiled the myth. It's more picturesque the way it is.'

'Death rather than dishonour,' Rod said pompously.

Lena let the observation pass in silence, a silence broken as they floated past the island by the chattering of the rosellas; the little red and green parrots who were flying from tree to tree before settling down for the night. The crimson sky, the luminous river, the little birds like flying flowers—it could all have been so beautiful if Rod, hard-eyed and cynical, had not destroyed the mood.

With a savage movement, as if goaded, he started the engine and swung the launch out into mid-stream where it clattered noisily on its way, shattering the evening's peace. Presently he turned from the wheel to glance at the girl in the stern with the sleeping child in her arms.

He said brusquely, 'Don't let her get too fond of you. Lena. It isn't kind.'

Stung by his tone, disarmed by her own private agreement as to the wisdom of his words, she made no answer.

'Taking her into your bed with you at nights,' he went on.

'It's mostly in the early mornings,' Lena interrupted rather irrelevantly—as though the time made any difference.

Rod shrugged. 'No matter when it is, it isn't wise. She's got to lose you before so long and we mustn't make the break any harder than it has to be.'

They were approaching the Windara bank now and as though a light had been turned off the crimson glory vanished suddenly from the sky. Now the dense miles of bush on either side of the river seemed to take over, dark, menacing, a powerful force waiting to engulf the scatter of human beings who lived on its edge.

It was eerie, Lena felt, as they disembarked. and she was glad to see the estate car waiting for them with its reassuring promise of headlights. Rod carried the sleeping child to the car, Lena following along the rough track. Somewhere in the bush a kookaburra uttered his mocking laughter.

Footnote to a perfect day, Lena thought ironically. She saw the light in the house on the hill above them and wondered how she was going to survive the weeks which still had to be lived through before she could leave Windara.

CHAPTER VIII

The following morning, having left Mandy at school, Lena took the two cheques to the bank on the main street. Mr Bexley, the chief accountant, greeted her warmly as she was shown into his office.

'I asked to see you specially, Mr Bexley,' she explained, 'because there are one or two questions I want to ask you.'

'Ask away, Miss Shannon!' he invited cordially. He held out a chair for her, facing his desk. He was a deeply tanned giant of a young man clad in the invariable spotless white short-sleeved shirt and snowy pants. The effect was of gleaming cleanliness.

'This money my uncle left me,' Lena began. 'It's coming to me in instalments at the moment and it's accumulating. I was wondering if there would be any difficulty in transferring it to England when I go back there in a few weeks' time?'

'None whatever. There are certain formalities and charges, of course, but it can be arranged through the bank.' He looked at her keenly across the desk. 'I'm sorry to hear you're thinking of leaving us so soon. Doesn't Australia appeal to you?'

Australians, Lena had discovered, were apt to be a little sensitive about a foreigner's reaction to their beloved country. You were supposed to find it a better place to live in than anywhere else in the world. What had 'poor little old England' got that Australia couldn't offer? Plus a hundred benefits such as an escape from the eternal fogs of the north and the long dark winters. Having heard all this from Mrs Clarens Lena was prepared for the implications of Mr Bexley's question.

'Of course Australia appeals to me,' she agreed. 'What I've seen of it is wonderful. But my home . . . my work . . . is in England.'

'So you aren't settling at Windara?'

Lena shook her head, wondering how much he might know about Uncle Tom's strange will. Even if the contents of it had been kept a secret there was bound, she thought, not for the first time, to have been speculation over it in the small community.

'My uncle's estate has been left to a distant cousin who lives in New Zealand,' she said. 'My visit here was planned before my uncle's last illness and I arrived in Brisbane not knowing of his death. I learned from his solicitor that since he had invited me to Windara he was anxious for me to stay here a while. It was one of his last wishes,' she improvised, and knew that in substance the statement was true. Just why he had wanted her to stay was her own business . . . and Rod's.

'But my work is in England,' she reiterated.

'Your work?' Mr Bexley demanded, frankly interested.

'I have secretarial qualifications,' Lena told him, and saw his rather too warmly intent glance light up.

'You wouldn't have any difficulty in finding secretarial jobs in Australia. In fact we could do with you right here in the bank, where we seem to be perennially short of clerking staff.'

Startled, she murmured that it was kind of him to make the suggestion. 'But at the moment my best course would seem to be to . . . go home.' She hesitated a little over this pronouncement. Home? A lonely bed-sitter in Earl's Court?

'Well, think about it,' Mr Bexley advised. 'And let me know if you change your mind. Queensland is an up-and-coming place and has almost continuous sun-shine, as well as the most glorious surfing beaches in the world. Have you done any surfing yet?'

'A little, but I'm not very good at it,' Lena admitted. There hadn't been any opportunities to practise the difficult art since the bush fire, with Rod busy on the farm.

'Now about this transfer of currency,' Mr Bexley began. For the rest of the interview they talked techni-calities. When the visit was over he showed her out with an almost courtly grace, taking her to the quite imposing entrance, opening the ornate swing doors for her and bowing her on her way.

'There are plenty of Pete Fosters in Australia,' Rod had said. Potential husbands was what he had meant. If, he had implied, a husband was what she was look-ing for. Was Mr Bexley one of the possibilities? She shrugged the thought away, mildly amused by the good-looking young man's obvious interest in her.

She would have a cup of coffee in one of the attrac-tive cafés in the high street before going back to Win-dara, she decided, and turning a corner walked slap into Pete Foster. 'Talk of the devil!' she murmured to herself. He greeted her exuberantly, so delighted to see her that after his first words of greeting he seemed tongue-tied and oddly awkward.

'I was just going to have a cup of coffee before going home.' she said, to make conversation.

'Do better, and stay and have lunch with me,' Pete urged. 'It's almost noon now and we could have a pre-lunch noggin instead of your coffee. Have you ever been to our five-star hotel? It's quite a place . . .' he was talking a little too quickly now, as if to ward off her possible refusal of his invitation. But she was, she discovered, not going to refuse it. A meal with

137

the friendly Pete would be more fun than the lonely run back to Windara followed by a lunch of sandwiches and strong tea with Mrs Clarens in the kitchen alcove.

'I should love to have lunch with you—thanks very much,' she said.

Pete's brown face lit up. 'Thank *you*!' he emphasised. 'You'll be doing me a great honour. Let's get going!' With a light hand under her elbow he steered her across the busy street and after a brief walk they came to the Southern Cross Hotel, a colonial style building set in a green garden dotted with jacaranda trees.

'My lucky trees!' Lena exclaimed when she found herself seated on a wide, raised verandah looking out over the flower-filled garden. 'I think it must be their heavenly blue colour, but they always make me feel good. There's a beautiful jacaranda outside my bedroom window at Windara.' So often she had looked out at it for its strange comfort.

'And you're happy at Windara?' Pete asked, gazing at her intently. almost pleadingly. Did he want her to be happy at Windara?

'I'm not entirely happy some of the time,' she admitted. 'It was sad to arrive there and not to find my uncle there to welcome me. His death was a shock. He had invited me out for a visit, you know. . . .'

Pete nodded seriously. 'Yes, I did know. It must have been hard for you arriving at Brisbane to hear of his sudden death.'

'It was,' Lena confirmed. 'But Mrs Clarens . . . and Rod,' she hesitated a little self-consciously over his name, 'have been very kind.'

'What else *could* they be?' Pete demanded, giving her a glance so highly charged with unspoken things that her own glance faltered and fell before it.

'You haven't been at Doora Heads the last couple of Sundays,' he reproached her. 'I've been there looking for you, hoping to see you.'

Lena drank a little of the fresh pineapple juice which she had insisted was more to her taste at this hour than anything stronger. Pineapples grown perhaps on the Windara hillside.

'Rod has been too busy clearing up after the fire to go surfing,' she explained.

Pete shook a sympathetic head. 'Bad business, that bush fire. But if you want to go surfing at the week ends I could always take you.' Colouring a little under his tan, he added, 'That is, if I wouldn't be butting in. I wouldn't want to muscle in on old Rod's territory.' There was no mistaking his meaning.

Lena forced a laugh which she hoped was convincingly lighthearted. 'Oh, there isn't anything like that in the offing. Rod and I are good friends, but there's nothing more, and not likely to be.'

Pete gave a sigh of relief, pondered a moment and puckering his brow said without any subtlety, 'I suppose that means there's someone waiting for you back home in England?'

Lena took a deep breath and brought out a very definite, 'No. There's no one in England or anywhere else. I'm heartwhole and fancy free.' If only that were the truth!

'Good!' Pete exulted. 'So the coast is clear.'

'I didn't quite mean that,' Lena laughed. In spite of herself she was enjoying this pathetically clumsy inquisition, because there was a genuine warmth and feeling behind it. Pete was so young and eager in his anxiety to make some contact with her, but doing it with such a lack of finesse that she found it appealing.

'I know I'm talking out of turn,' he was saying. 'It's

all a bit too soon, isn't it? You hardly know me. But that can be remedied.' He leaned across the small wicker table separating them. 'I'm crazy about you, Lena,' he declared, throwing caution to the winds. 'You may as well know it—I fell in love with you hopelessly and for ever that day I fished you out from under the breakers.'

An announcement which sobered her, took the laughter from her eyes. Poor Pete! Though she wouldn't quite admit it to herself, his obvious adoration was balm to her wounded spirit. But it was more than balm for a wounded spirit she wanted from life.

She said gently, putting her hand out to him, 'It's no use, Pete. It wasn't quite true what I said just now. I'm not really heartwhole. The truth is that I've got my love life a bit snarled up, having fallen in love with the wrong man.'

'Was that what drove you out to Australia?'

She left the question unanswered, vaguely aware of relief that Pete should have jumped to the conclusion that her unhappy attachment was to an Englishman. Let Pete Foster jump to any conclusions he pleased. Deliberately she concentrated on the delicious dessert with which they were ending the meal, a mixture of fresh local fruits of exotic variety, spiced with a dash of Kirsch. She felt relaxed, a little sleepy in the early afternoon heat after the excellent lunch. Beyond the verandah the garden lay bathed in golden light. She looked at it through the branches of the jacaranda trees with their blue flowers which always seemed to her the colour of hope. But hope, she remembered, could die, and already the blue blossoms were falling in masses to the ground.

With a sigh she recalled herself to the realities of life. 'I ought to be getting back to Windara. Mrs

Clarens will be wondering where I've got to.'

'She'll guess you've run into a friend,' Pete suggested easily. 'It's long past two o'clock already. You might as well wait in Latonga until it's time for you to collect Mandy from school.'

So he knew her routine. Had he, she wondered, been watching her comings and goings to the little town?

'You could come and have a look round my pad,' he was suggesting . . . the large bright ultra-modern car sales room and garage at the end of the high street.

She went with him because at the moment it seemed the inevitable thing to do. It would be foolish to go all the way up the river to Windara, only to turn round almost at once and come back again to fetch Mandy.

The car showroom when they reached it was impressive with its array of shining, luxury cars—an indication surely of the prosperity of the district. When he had showed her proudly all he thought would interest her he invited her to come upstairs to the spacious flat above and meet his mother, who proved to be a small, dainty little woman with a kindly smile which made Lena instantly welcome. Her handclasp was warm, her glance keenly interested.

'Tom Shannon's niece . . . I've heard of you. Pete has spoken of you. It was good of you to come and see us. I hope you'll come again . . . just pop in whenever you're passing.'

She was sorry Lena could not wait for afternoon tea, but it was already time to be making for Mandy's school. Pete insisted on accompanying her.

'I'm planning to build myself a house on the outskirts of the town,' he told her, as he walked by her side. 'Mum would probably prefer to stay on at the flat, specially if I marry. . . .'

His silence throbbed with unspoken questions.

'I know it's too soon to be definite about anything,' he brought out at last, 'but if you'd like to look at the plans of the house some time . . . drive out with me and see the site. . . .'

'You take my breath away, Pete!' Lena laughed.

'I know. I'm a clumsy so-and-so. But I feel as if I've known you for ages.'

'Only the sad truth is that you don't know me at all,' she reminded him.

'That could be remedied, if only you'd let me go on seeing you. I would give you all the time you want in which to make up your mind.'

It was as if he were selling her one of his luxury cars.

'Please, Pete!' she expostulated. 'It's no use. Can't we just be good friends?'

'Sure we can,' he agreed heartily. 'I'll go along with anything you say. Maybe in time. . . .' He left the sentence unfinished with a shrug. 'Meanwhile, what about a trip to the surfing beach next Sunday?' He waited so anxiously for her reply that she found herself accepting the invitation. Besides, another try at surfing would be fun. Sundays at Windara with Rod absent in the fields was oddly lonely, even with Mrs Clarens and Mandy and the ponies for company. During the week there were the daily trips to town, but at the weekends there was too much time to think, and she would wander about the big shabby house wishing she had been more involved with its upkeep. There was so much that needed doing. But even when she had suggested spring-cleaning the office Rod had said it was hardly worth the trouble. 'It will be no time at all before we shall be leaving it,' he had reminded her. 'Let the New Zealand cousin paint it and re-furbish it if he wants to.'

142

Pete, delighted with her promise to go surfing with him, left her at the school gate where she was soon surrounded by lively children, dancing around her like puppies newly released from captivity. Mandy was full of some project she was engaged upon—a picture she was to make on a piece of perforated canvas with multi-coloured wools. She talked about it excitedly as they chug-chugged up the sleepy river, the afternoon sun blazing down on them. To Lena's surprise Rod was waiting for them on the landing stage.

'Where on earth have you been?' he greeted Lena angrily. 'I've been worried sick about you since Mrs Clarens told me you hadn't come home to lunch. I began to think you must have come to grief on the river and was just about to set out to look for you.' He indicated a small row boat tied up at the end of the wharf.

Mandy had scrambled ashore, eagerly telling her father about her wool picture. He hardly listened to her, holding a hand out automatically to help Lena to alight from the launch.

'I met Pete Foster in town and had lunch with him,' she explained reluctantly. Rod's face was a thunder-cloud.

'So that's what held you up! I needn't have troubled myself.'

'No,' she confirmed tersely, 'you needn't.'

He had brought the estate car which would save them the rough if short walk up the lane. The train with its load of sugar cane came rattling into view as they stood by the car. The driver of the train stopped at the sight of Rod and there was an exchange of greetings, comments on the load of cane, congratulatory remarks over the amount they had been able to save from the ravages of the fire.

It reminded Lena of the day she had arrived at Windara and the men on the sugar train had stopped to greet them, and how this had led to her discovery of Rod's true identity. Anger against him revived as she remembered the deception he had played on her that day, and how he had laughed at her discomfiture. The recollection helped to harden her heart against him as they went rattling over the uneven ground in the estate car. His face was set and grim, and presently he turned to her, saying over Mandy's curly head, ' Don't ever go off for hours like that again without telling Mrs Clarens or myself what your plans may be . . . not even for the sake of the alluring Pete Foster.'

' He's not alluring,' she snapped crossly. ' And surely you and Mrs Clarens don't have to get all worked up if I stay around Latonga for a while sometimes. I might want to do some shopping . . . or have my hair done. . . .'

' You could let us know.'

' Why?' she persisted. ' Nothing could possibly happen to me in a safe place like Latonga.'

' The river isn't Latonga, and it's partly in flood since that heavy rain a couple of weeks ago.'

' And I could get drowned like the beautiful love-sick Caloola,' she mocked.

He did not answer, but the look he flashed at her was livid. After a frosty silence he said, ' Please don't let me interfere with your meetings with Pete. But there are such things as telephones. You could have given Mrs Clarens a call today. There she was, waiting lunch for you. . . .'

' I'm sorry,' Lena brought out unwillingly. Really, Rod was being ridiculous! Talking about lunch as if it were some Lucullan feast which would have spoiled. A little cold meat, in all probability, or some bread and cheese and fresh fruit. That was all they usually bothered about in the middle of a hot day at Windara.

The days which followed fell into their usual quiet and sometimes lonely routine. Rod was more and more elusive. There was just Mrs Clarens and Mandy . . and the kitten Goldie who had developed a marked affection for Lena and followed her from room to room, purring expectantly. Mandy adored it and Lena would wonder with a heavy heart what would happen to Goldie when the break-up of the household came, and how Mandy would bear her parting from her pet. For it was unlikely they would be able to take it with them if they went to live in a city.

If she married Pete, she thought crazily, she would be able to offer the kitten a home. But you didn't marry someone who couldn't possibly matter to you in order to comfort a small stray cat. All the same, there floated vaguely in her mind the thought that there were other possibilities in life besides a return to a bed-sitter in London. And they had nothing to do with Rod Carron. Life didn't begin and end with Rod. There could be other reasons for remaining in Queensland besides Uncle Tom's crazy will. Hadn't Mr Bexley at the bank offered her a job? Salaries were good in Australia. She might even be able to afford to live at the Southern Cross hotel and eat lunch every day looking out at the flowering garden. Pete would take her surfing at the weekends. There would be other young men. Mr Bexley perhaps . . . her thoughts rambled on. Rod and Mandy would have vanished from the picture. In time she would get over the pain of that. She would *have* to. Life went on. You had to do the best you could with it, press on, cutting your losses.

These sensible reflections, however, were oddly unconvincing. But by the weekend she found herself looking forward to her trip to the surfing beach with Pete. When she announced her plan at breakfast time on Sunday, Rod received the news in silence. It was Mandy who piped up, 'I thought you were coming with Daddy and me.'

Lena turned to Rod in some bewilderment. 'I'm taking a day off from the field work,' he told her. 'And I'd promised Mandy a picnic at Waronga, that's the beach the other side of Doora Heads, where the water comes in gently and there are no great breakers; it's a favourite bathing place for children. It did occur to me that you might like to come with us, but don't let me interfere with your arrangements.'

Lena was thrown into a state of emotional confusion. Why had she promised to go surfing with Pete before finding out Rod's Sunday project? But she had assumed he would, as usual, be still engrossed with his sugar cane salvaging.

'I can easily put Pete off,' she offered wildly. 'As a matter of fact some gentle exercise in a manageable sea would suit me much better than another tussle with the great breakers at Doora.'

Rod's glance was scornful. 'Don't be childish, Lena. If you've fixed to go to Doora with Pete for heaven's sake get on with it. Mandy and I will be perfectly contented with each other's company. Won't we, poppet?' He put an arm around the little girl who was leaning against his chair.

They were happy on their own before I came, Lena thought achingly. They'll be happy after I leave. . . .

The incident spoiled the blue and golden day for her, although Pete was everything an escort could possibly have been, collecting her in his luxurious car at the appointed time. Luckily Rod and Mandy had already departed for Waronga, avoiding what might have been an awkward encounter.

The weather was perfect, hot and brilliant, with just enough breeze to whip up the great jade green waves with their combing white tops. And Pete was an adept instructor. Under his tuition Lena felt she was making real progress with her surfing.

During a picnic lunch on the beach they were joined by other young people, girls and men, acquaintances of Pete's, all of them keen surfers. So that the afternoon session was hilarious—a relief to Lena since it tended to break up the intimacy which had been developing in the morning between herself and Pete. Being taught how to surf by a virile young man wasn't exactly a decorous exercise. Time and again Pete had to rescue his pupil bodily from the churning tide, carrying her to the shore where she could recover her breath . . . and her surfing board. If at times he was reluctant to release her from his enforced embrace she tried not to notice it. In the clamour of the waves and the moments of real danger which were inevitable with someone as unskilled as herself an amorous mood was not easy to achieve. At least she hoped that was how Pete was finding it. It was certainly true for her. Pete was her lifeline, no more. Nor, she realised, could it have been otherwise. In spite of his obvious delight in their physical contacts, in spite of his splendid physique, so completely revealed as he rode the great waves, the magic was missing. If it had been Rod now. . . . But Lena thrust the thought firmly aside. That way lay too much pain. The surfing was exciting, wonderful . . . she must not let Rod spoil it for her. She must get the best out of this day on a beautiful Pacific beach, thirteen thousand miles away from London bed-sitters.

By the time Pete drove her back to Windara they were both happily tired, relaxing peacefully in one another's company. But Lena was relieved when Pete refused her invitation to come into the house before returning to Latonga.

He ought to get back to his mother, he said. She had been alone all day. Lena liked him for his concern. In fact in many ways she liked Pete Foster very much indeed. But that was as far as it went. Now as she entered the house her whole being seemed to come alive at the sound of Rod's voice. He greeted her with unexpected ease and good humour, enquiring what sort of a day she had had and how the surfing was coming along. He and Mandy, it emerged, had enjoyed their quieter time at Waronga.

'I've just been putting her to bed,' he said. 'She wants you to go up and tuck her in and kiss her goodnight. And don't forget,' he called after Lena as she started up the stairs, 'to make sure Goldie isn't hidden beneath the bedclothes!' Separating Mandy and Goldie was a nightly game played with zest and good humour by the purring kitten as well as his little mistress. He would burrow deeper and deeper beneath the covers while Lena pursued him to the accompaniment of Mandy's delighted laughter.

Tonight Lena gave herself up to the homely ritual, not letting herself think of the time so soon to come when Mandy and Goldie and herself would be relentlessly separated.

It was two evenings later when Rod, coming in earlier than usual from the fields, asked Lena if she would care to come and have a spot of dinner with him at the Silver Beach Hotel. She was so taken aback that for a moment she could not find her voice to answer

148

him. The world seemed to whirl about her. Furious with herself for her reaction, she rallied her common sense, forcing herself to say quietly that it would be fun to go to the Silver Beach and she would love it.

But why, why was he suggesting it? This hard-headed, self-contained young man who regarded her simply as an embarrassing adjunct to Tom Shannon's equivocal legacy.

'I feel it's time you and I had a little talk,' he was saying. 'There are things I want to say to you.'

What things? What could he possibly have to say? She abandoned speculation and went upstairs to make herself ready, putting on the backless white dress she had worn at the memorable dance. Perhaps it wasn't altogether suitable for the occasion, but the night was sultry and the dress feather-light. Also, with her beautifully tanned back to display, it was the most becoming garment she possessed. After her days on the beach she was almost as deep a golden brown as Rod himself. Clad in a white linen dinner jacket and casual slacks, he conducted her rather ceremoniously to the waiting car. There was an air of suppressed urgency about him, as if the things he had to say to her later were of some importance. Whatever could they be? She couldn't even begin to speculate, though at the bottom of her unruly heart mad little hopes were beginning to stir to life. Surely anything 'ordinary' could have been conveyed to her at Windara House or in the office. Why this drive through the warm, purple night to a luxury hotel some twenty miles away?

They drove for most of the journey in silence. There was no moon tonight, only the headlights to reveal the gleam of the river on one side of the road, the shadowy menace of the bush on the other. At one point a furry bundle like an outsize cat with a fat striped tail lurched out of the way of their wheels just in time.

'A possum!' Rod exclaimed. 'We used to have one living in the trees at Windara. He'd come down on to the lawn every evening as soon as it was dusk and beg for titbits. You'd have enjoyed making friends with him, but unfortunately he seems to have moved on to other hunting grounds, or given up the ghost. Your uncle was fond of it, made quite a pet of it. Strange that the little creature should have vanished at about the same time as he died. As if it knew . . .'

The simple story seemed to Lena to reveal the homely pleasant things which had gone on at Windara during her uncle's lifetime, a life in which Rod had shared.

She said impulsively, 'You must miss it all . . . my uncle, the possum . . . all the small happy things. . . .' Her voice faltered. There was a sudden lump in her throat.

'I've grown to mistrust happiness,' Rod said, and for the rest of the journey they spoke no more.

The restaurant at the hotel was as softly lit, as glamorous as it had been the first night they dined there. But this evening something was missing. Their conversation was desultory, even dull, as they ate the delicious food put before them. It wasn't until they had reached the coffee stage that Rod, having lit a soothing cigar, cleared his throat significantly and began:

'This matter I wanted to discuss with you, Lena. I hope you'll bear with me . . . hear me out before you offer any comment.' He puffed at his cigar, in an uneasy way, avoiding her glance. For a long moment he remained silent, as if unwilling to embark on what it was he had to say. Taking the cigar from his lips, he gazed at it blankly, then put it down on the waiting ash tray where, after the manner of unsmoked cigars, it promptly went out. It was as though some impassable barrier lay between them. Then suddenly his whole attention was upon her, riveting her. There was purpose now in his manner, a certain ruthlessness. If whatever he was about to say to her was difficult, he would not let that hinder him.

'During the past few weeks,' he began, 'I've been busy assessing the possibility of several jobs which might be available to me when I leave Windara. This week a suitable offer has been made to me by a firm in Sydney. The sort of job I used to do before I came to Windara . . . selling agricultural machinery.'

His eyes were all brilliant dark centres, looking at her across the candlelit table. 'Obviously they aren't going to wait weeks for me to make up my mind, I've got to give them an answer to their offer pretty soon.' The appeal in his glance now was desperate.

'You mean,' she helped him out, 'you don't want to finish the specified six months at Windara?'

He said in a low tone, and he wasn't looking at her any more, 'Apart from this job altogether I've had about as much as I can stand of Tom Shannon's strange will. I don't know about you . . .'

If it was a question Lena left it unanswered while her heart went small and cold. So this was the end of the road for them, and he couldn't be quick enough reaching it.

She watched him pick up the dead cigar and lay it down again. 'I wouldn't want you to suffer financially,' he said, 'if you agree to release me from our strange obligation. You ought to have your full share of the six months' money which was part to the arrangement to which I subscribed. I would gladly make it up to

151

you. I'm not penniless. There are shares I could sell. . . .'

'No, no!' she cried, her colour rising. 'I wouldn't dream of taking your money.'

'We can see how it works out,' Rod temporised. 'But I'm not going to take advantage of your generosity —be sure of that. However, I would probably be able to stay on and work at Windara for another month. My prospective employers will hardly expect me to throw up my current commitments at a moment's notice. With a bit of luck I may be able to fulfil at least half of the six months your uncle specified.

'Six months,' he mused then. 'The arbitrary period during which we were supposed to fall in love with one another.' There was mockery in his spurt of laughter. 'Didn't the old man know anything about love, or human nature? It doesn't take two normal people as a rule as long as six months to find out if they're indispensable to one another. Indeed the discovery can come at a first meeting, or very soon afterwards.'

She saw his jaw grow taut, and there was pain now in the dark-centred eyes. Was he thinking of Dolores?

She said, 'It's all right, Rod. I know you hate the way we've had to live during the past weeks. I've felt it more and more every day.'

'You mean you hate it too?'

It wasn't at all what she had meant, but she once more left his question unanswered.

'There's another angle to it,' he hurried on. 'If I go to Sydney it means Mandy and I can live with my parents. My mother will adore looking after Mandy during the periods I'm travelling around the State on my sales work.'

'But of course,' Lena agreed eagerly, genuinely relieved at this possible solution of the domestic side of

Rod's life, and Mandy's. 'You mustn't think of letting this chance slip through your fingers because of me. I can easily leave Windara at any time that suits you. I don't have to go back to England.'

'Pete?' he asked quickly.

She shook her head. 'Nothing so romantic. Mr Bexley at the bank when I told him I was a qualified secretary at once offered me a job.'

Rod's eyebrows shot up. 'Well, there you are! What could be better?' He sounded vastly relieved to be rid of her and her problems so simply.

'You could make Windara House your headquarters for some time, I should imagine, with old Mother Clarens for company. No need for either of you to clear out until after probate is granted, and that, I imagine, will take some while yet. And I don't suppose it will be all that easy to rustle up the New Zealand beneficiary. He'll have his own affairs to settle before he takes over at Windara. Meanwhile you wouldn't be lonely. Pete Foster would see to that. He's a good sort, is old Pete.'

'Will you stop marrying me off to Pete Foster!' Lena cried out, unable to endure any more.

'Okay,' Rod laughed. 'Don't blow your top. I wasn't probing. Only Pete is not to be sneered at as a prospective husband. There'd be plenty of lolly in the background. That's a pretty sound car business he has at Latonga.'

So Rod still thought of her as a gold-digger. Lena felt as if her heart could hold no more pain. 'Money means nothing to me,' she declared. 'Neither Pete's, nor yours.' Her voice shook. She had to concentrate on fighting back the tears. The final humiliation would be to break down in front of Rod, here in a public restaurant.

'Money is not to be despised,' Rod pointed out pontifically. 'At the same time, money gained in the way your uncle offered it to us could only have been disastrous—poisoning all trust between us. Your reaction of utter disgust at the whole scheme the first day we met was the healthy one. You despised me because you thought I was ready to compromise, grabbing at six months' easy money with the prospect of finding a permanent income and an acquiescent wife at the end of it.'

Remembering how bitterly she had turned on him the day he had met her at Latonga, she could find no words now to save the situation. 'It was because I felt you hadn't played fair with me,' she tried. 'Hiding your identity!'

'I know,' he nodded. 'Dirty Tricks Department. But as long as that damned Shannon money existed it would have come between us one way or another. We would never have made a go of it.'

'Even if we'd loved one another?' she whispered.

He did not choose to hear her, but glanced at his wrist watch, saying it was time they were hitting the road.

'As long as you approve of my accepting this job in Sydney,' he wrapped it up.

'I do,' she confirmed.

His unclouded smile rewarded her. She must try to be glad for him, seeing him happy because he was so easily shaking her off.

'I'll have a talk with McKindry about it all next week. Run into Brisbane and have a word with the old boy.' He was taking out his wallet, leaving a sheaf of dollar bills inside the folded account which had been left on a plate at his side.

Payment for a meal of dust and ashes, thought Lena

as she went with him out into the hot moonless night. There was thunder about, Rod hazarded. 'I hope it moves away. We've had about as much rain as we can take this season. Just when I'm getting the plantations back into shape another storm would be a blow.'

So he still cared about the land and the crops. The sugar canes and fruit he had worked so hard to save. Had he forgotten how soon he would be leaving it all?

Seated by his side in the big smoothly running car, Lena clenched her hands on her lap and stared blindly into the headlamp path which lay before them—a gleaming, illusory path with the blackness and menace of the night and the bush all around it.

CHAPTER IX

It was a relief to Lena to find herself in her own room at last. She moved about quietly so as not to disturb Mandy, who lay rosy and relaxed in the deep sleep of childhood.

Slipping out of the backless white gown, she hung it in the wardrobe, wishing she had not worn it. A less showy dress would have been more in keeping with the evening's matter-of-fact mood. Rod had invited her to the Silver Beach to ensure her co-operation in his early departure from Windara. What else, in heaven's name, had she expected?

Lying in bed she faced the vacuum which lay ahead of her. That job in the bank with the nice Mr Bexley now seemed wholly improbable. Pete Foster and his ingenuous offers of marriage, complete with a glittering car sales business and a newly built home, seemed even more improbable. Projects for which she could never have had any real heart. A London bed-sitter loomed like a dull grey haven, but still a haven. Should she write to Deborah and Susan, the girls with whom she had shared her last flat? Or would it be possible to move to Sydney and get a job there? In that way she would see something more of the great Australian continent before returning to England. But her inward laughter was bitter. It wasn't the great Australian continent which lured her, but Rod. If she were working in Sydney at least he would be in the same city.

Oh, but this was crazy! she told herself, turning over on her pillow and making a determined effort to get off to sleep. By this time, however, the thunder

156

Rod had dreaded was beginning to rumble in the distance, soon developing into a full-scale storm of the most violent Queensland intensity. Whiplashes of lightning seemed to scorch the window. The noise overhead was deafening, as though the very citadels of heaven were being blown up by some unimaginably ferocious celestial artillery.

'May I come into your bed?' came a small voice from the other end of the room. 'I'm scared!'

Lena turned on the bedside light and without waiting for permission Mandy ran across the floor and flung herself into the arms Lena held out to her.

'Better not have her in your bed . . . she's getting far too fond of you,' Rod's warning echoed. But tonight surely was an exception?

They lay down together, Mandy with her head on Lena's shoulder, and even before the storm had rolled away the little girl was trustfully sleeping. It was some time before Lena could follow her example.

Following on the days of intense heat, the storm seemed to have broken the weather pattern permanently. The occasional nightly showers now intruded into the daylight hours, though even now, in spite of the intensity of the rain, intervals of drying sunlight and heat helped to save what was left of the sugar cane and fruit crops. Rod, undeterred either by the weather or the uncertainty of his plans, continued to toil from dawn till dusk in the fields alongside his workers. The new canes, planted after the fire, needed constant attention; the surviving pineapples and strawberries were ready for harvesting.

One morning when Lena was helping Mrs Clarens in the kitchen Rod arrived with a large basket of the ripe scarlet berries.

'I thought you might like to do something with

these,' he told Mrs Clarens. 'Bottle them, or make them into jam. They're in perfect condition at the moment, but another night or two of these recurring storms and the crop will be useless.'

There was a heavy silence for a moment, then Rod, sensing its meaning, shrugged and turned away.

'There'll be none of us here a few weeks from now to eat bottled strawberries,' Mrs Clarens brought out in a grudging tone.

'Okay. For the moment I'd forgotten that.' He gave the basket on the table a small vicious push. 'Throw them down the drain, give them to the birds . . . do what you like with them!' He walked out, slamming the screen door behind him angrily.

Mrs Clarens and Lena looked at one another gloomily.

'They mustn't be wasted,' Mrs Clarens said at last. 'Rod could take them back to the fields and give them to the pickers to take home. I could save a few for a strawberry flan, and we could have some with cream for lunch. Mandy loves them.' She rose and fetched a glass dish from the dresser.

'So you know about Rod's prospective job in Sydney,' Lena brought out a trifle nervously. So far she and Mrs Clarens had not discussed the immediate future of the residents of Windara, since Lena was not sure if Rod would have spoken of his plans yet to the housekeeper.

But now she was saying, 'Yes, he told me about it the other day. A right shock it was. But I suppose it had to come sooner or later.' Absently she bit into a strawberry. 'A pity,' she added tersely, 'you and he couldn't have made a go of it, the way Tom Shannon hoped. But there it is. . . .' She shrugged her resignation. 'Sometimes I think Rod buried his heart with Dolores. But seven years is a long time. He ought to be getting over her death by now . . . and thinking of marrying again, even if it was just for Mandy's sake. The child needs mothering. Every child that age does.'

Lena felt the words float over her, pushing them away from her, trying not to hear them. 'What are you going to do when Windara breaks up?' she asked Mrs Clarens.

The older woman sighed. 'I have a brother in Melbourne I could go to. But I'm not really keen on it. I don't get on all that well with his wife. All the same, it would be somewhere to stay while I look for another job. Indeed,' she added, her voice rising hopefully, 'I might get a job right here. The New Zealand cousin who's taking over might want me to housekeep for him.

'What about you?' she flung at Lena then. 'What will you do?'

Gulping down the strawberry she had just put in her mouth, Lena heard herself say, 'Oh, I expect I shall be going back to England.'

Mrs Clarens nodded as though this were the inevitable answer. 'All your friends are there, I guess . . . your own people.'

'My aunt,' Lena said, trying to make it sound enthusiastic—the remote if kindly aunt who had never really played an important role in her life. 'I must write to her,' she added listlessly. 'And to the girls with whom I shared a flat in London. I don't know how they'll be fixed by now, if they'll have room for me.'

But Mrs Clarens seemed to have lost interest and didn't appear to be listening any more. 'All these berries,' she sighed. 'Seems such a waste.

'It's *all* a waste,' she added in a goaded tone. 'You

going off back to England when you could have made such a lovely little wife for Rod if only he could have seen it that way.'

'Don't!' Lena stopped her. 'Leave it alone. It just didn't work out, that's all. There was my side of it too, don't forget.' She had to add that to bolster her pride.

Mrs Clarens nodded. 'Sorry if I was being a bit too personal. I didn't mean any offence, I'm sure. I guess there will be a young man waiting for you back home.'

An assumption Lena didn't bother to correct, changing the subject firmly by saying, 'If I eat any more of these gorgeous strawberries I shan't want any lunch.'

When she had washed the fruit stains from her hands she went up to her room and got out her writing pad. It would be no harm to contact Aunt Mary, and her flatmates, let them know she was thinking of returning to England. They wouldn't be surprised since they had never expected her to remain in Australia indefinitely. She had not told either her relatives or her friends about the strange contents of Uncle Tom's will, and they had naturally assumed she was staying on in Queensland just for a holiday.

When she had written the letters and folded them, a feeling of relief came to her, as if in sealing the aerogrammes she had sealed her fate. Of course she would return to England. It was the only sensible thing to do. Pete Foster and Mr Bexley were cardboard figures, totally unreal. And Rod, far from being a cardboard figure, was so agonisingly real that the sooner she put the width of the world between them, the better! Outside her window the jacaranda tree was covered with new little crumpled green leaves. The last of the blue flowers had fallen. It was a fitting symbol.

Just before lunch she took the aerogrammes down to the office, meaning to give them to the postman if he came. But Rod, busy at the desk, looked up as she entered. 'Any letters for the post?' he asked, glancing at the blue folders in her hand. 'I'm going in to Latonga this afternoon to pick up a new tyre for the estate car and can fetch Mandy from school, saving you the trip.'

She handed him the aerogrammes, with a murmured, 'Thanks. I'll be glad when they're on their way. They are to my aunt and my old flatmates,' she added. 'I've told them I'm coming back.' It was like plunging off a great height, saying the words aloud, confirming her departure. Telling Rod seemed to seal the arrangement irrevocably. She was going. Soon she would be free from Windara, Rod, everything to do with the pain which possessed her.

'So you're leaving us,' he said. 'Turning your back on Aussie land and all it has to offer you. A job in the local bank . . . Pete Foster! Pood Pete, he'll be heartbroken.' He flashed her a glance in which, strangely, anger seemed to burn. Perhaps because she was spurning his country . . . and Pete, his countryman.

'Yes, I'm going home,' she reiterated flatly. 'It seems the best thing to do.'

'You're probably right.' His voice was uninterested now, as he returned to the work before him on the desk. He didn't really care whether she went or stayed. It made no difference to him. But when suddenly he looked up at her again with the fateful letters in his hand, his eyes were strangely alight. It was as if he had touched her, so intimate was his glance.

A momentary illusion, a moment which quickly passed, might never have been.

Once more lying awake that night, Lena wondered

how soon she would be able to set off for England. There was really nothing to hinder her leaving almost at once. Rod might be staying on for another few weeks, but there was no reason why she should wait for his departure. She would write to Mr McKindry tomorrow, telling him of her decision. No doubt that would be the end of her share in the Shannon legacy. But that was a detail which troubled her not at all. If only the other considerations hurt her as little! For it wasn't only Rod she would be leaving, but Mandy whom she had grown to love very dearly. The daily life at Windara had wound itself round her lonely heart—all the little things; the kitten, the ponies, having Mandy to sleep in her room. It was the nearest approach to a home that she had known since her mother died. She would miss it all terribly.

And the country itself . . . the wild beauty of Queensland with its blazing sunshine and scarlet sunsets, its endless miles of mysterious bushland where every sort of gum tree grew; the red, the ghostly-stemmed white —there were, Rod had told her, some four hundred species—enough to take over the entire continent! There was the river too; when she was miles away she would remember her daily trips on its wild green waters. She would think of the swans, the ibises, the cranes, the little rosellas. And she would miss the friendly people, the gay little coastal towns beside the surfing beaches. Oh, those beaches with the blue-green waves rolling in on them!

She would say goodbye to it all.

Turning and twisting on her pillow, she tried to sleep, but by now the nightly thunder was rumbling away over the river and the mangrove swamps. Soon the rain was falling, a hissing torrent of water to wash the earth from the newly planted canes over which

Rod had toiled so faithfully ever since the night of the fire.

It was late when at last she slept, but she woke as the sun rose, as golden and shameless as though rain and thunder clouds were unknown. A tempestuous climate of extremes, somehow it matched this great unconquered continent.

Getting out of bed, she set about composing her all-important letter to Mr McKindry. She would post it when she took Mandy to school. But when she went down to breakfast it was to discover that Rod had decided to take Mandy to school by car. He didn't like the look of the river, he said. It seemed to him a bit too swollen for safety after the night's heavy rain. He did not ask Lena if she would like to accompany them and she found she could not suggest it herself. It was ridiculous how important everything Rod did or did not do with regard to herself had become. But there it was; she could not help being hyper-sensitive to his every mood and action.

She was reluctant to ask him to post her letter to Mr McKindry. He might have asked questions about its contents, which she would have found difficult to answer. She had told him she was returning to England, but she had not made it clear that she was going almost at once. Would that matter to him? No doubt it would be a relief.

Down in the office a little later she decided to re-write Mr McKindry's letter and type it. The first draft did not quite satisfy her. It was not an easy letter to compose—a confession that she was unable to fulfil her part of the bargain Uncle Tom had made in his will. She would say nothing about Rod's decision to back out. He must speak for himself. Perhaps, she thought, he had already done so—though he had not yet been to Brisbane to consult the solicitor, a course he had spoken of that night at the Silver Beach hotel. It would make her own approach to the old man easier if he had heard Rod's side of the situation.

But once more her tongue was tied. She couldn't ask Rod outright if he had been in touch with Mr McKindry by letter or phone about their mutual rejection of the terms of the will. What was the matter with her? Once more the thought of his reaction to any further discussion about the will scared her into silence. It was so unlike her. Never in her life before had she been afraid of anyone in this way. Though it wasn't exactly fear where Rod was concerned, she corrected herself. It was just that he mattered too much.

The morning hours passed quickly. There was some work to be done in the office, pay packets to be made up, a few letters to answer—mostly attempts to placate customers who had had to be kept waiting for deliveries of fruit or sugar cane, owing to the fire.

When she returned to the house for lunch Mrs Clarens told her Rod had phoned to say he would be staying in Latonga until late afternoon as he had some business to attend to there. This meant he would be bringing Mandy back from school, Mrs Clarens enlarged.

So there would be no need, Lena realised, for her afternoon trip to Latonga where she had been planning to post Mr McKindry's letter. Fate seemed to be conspiring against her sending it on its way.

The midday heat by this time had become almost unbearable, so that when they had finished their lunch both women retired to lounge chairs on the shaded verandah to rest a while, the kitten joining them to curl up on Lena's lap. Tired after her disturbed night, she slept. When she woke with a start some time later both Mrs Clarens and the kitten had disappeared. She looked at her watch and saw that it was half past three. The last post left Latonga round about five. If she took the launch down the river she would be easily able to catch it, despatching not only Mr McKindry's letters but those she had written in the office during the morning.

Hurrying into the house to fetch her handbag, she supposed she had better tell Mrs Clarens where she was going . . . remembering the fuss Rod had made the time she had stayed in Latonga to lunch with Pete Foster. He had resented her unexplained absence, saying he was nervous for her when she was on the river. Would he approve of her negotiating it today? He had spoken of its swollen currents, but that was in the early morning. Since then the land had dried out and presumably the volume of water in the river too would have fallen. Anyway, river or no river, she was going to post Mr McKindry's letter. Rod's inclination to fuss about her movements could be a mild sort of tyranny . . . male aggression. It certainly wasn't brought about by any kind of tender concern!

Mrs Clarens was nowhere to be found. Sometimes during the afternoon she would go up to the strawberry fields to talk with the women pickers. To go and look for her would take up too much valuable time, so Lena scribbled a note for her, explaining her absence, and left it in a conspicuous place on the kitchen table.

The sky, she noticed, as she ran down to the river, was a queer coppery colour. A profound hush lay over the land and water. Not a leaf stirred in the endless ranks of gum trees which lined the river banks. It would be a relief to get out into mid-stream. It took her a little while to untie the covers which had protected the open deck of the launch from the night's rain, but at last she was on her way.

Going downstream the steering was easy. There was an oily calm on the water, not a ripple to be seen. She reached the landing stage at Latonga without incident and hurried to the post office with her precious letter. The post office was a fair distance from the school, but in any case there would be no point in calling there; Rod and Mandy would already be well on their way home by road. She decided to have a cup of tea before starting her own journey back to Windara.

The coppery sky had turned grey by the time she reached the river, the strange calm still prevailed. It would make her return journey easy, she thought. But as she moved out into mid-stream she could feel the power of the current against which she was moving. It was with difficulty that she held on to the steering wheel. She would, she decided, try to keep in the lee of the offside bank, the one that was most heavily wooded. The thick trees and bushes there would surely give her some shelter. But it was not much easier, she found, and her progress was slow and difficult.

Presently she realised, with a stirring alarm, that it wasn't only the overcast sky which was making it dark. The brief tropical twilight was upon her. She had lingered longer than was wise over that cup of tea. It was breathlessly hot and the strange calm on the water now seemed to mock her as the swollen currents blocked her way. The world with its dark motionless trees seemed strangely deserted. There was not a bird or any living creature in sight. This was the hour when the rosellas—the little red and green parrots—should have been chattering in the trees, arranging their sleeping places. But there wasn't one to be seen.

As she rounded a bend Lena could see the island of

Caloola looming ahead. That meant she was about half way home. If only she could beat the rapidly gathering darkness! How would she manage the boat without light? Tonight there would not be the glimmer of stars to guide her. Rod would be furious—justifiably—if anything happened to harm his precious launch, a reflection which did nothing to raise her sinking spirits. She felt so small and alone chug-chugging along in the gloom. Already she had difficulty in seeing the bank on the far side of the river, and the currents tugging at her prow seemed to be increasing in intensity.

However, she had almost reached the island now, she cheered herself. She could make out the mass of the great central rock—the sacrificial stone, where strange unspeakable rites had been performed in ancient times. The thought brought a shiver down her spine. Though she wouldn't admit it to herself, she was beginning to be pretty scared.

Then, between one moment and the next, with unbelievable suddenness, catastrophe struck.

Violent as a physical assault the great wind came screaming up-river from the direction of the ocean. Within seconds the water was a churning fury, lashed by the power of the cyclone—for this complete disintegration of the elements could be nothing less. Terrified beyond coherent thought, Lena clung to the wheel, which no longer seemed to have any control over the tossing craft. The whole launch leaped about like a bucking bronco, and after a brief interval the wheel was wrenched from her grasp and she was flung face downwards on the deck. She could feel the launch going round and round as if caught in a whirlpool. It could only be a matter of moments before it sank.

And all the while the shrill screaming of the wind

roared in her ears, mingled with the whining and crashing of the storm-tossed trees. She heard herself whimper—utterly abandoned now to sheer terror. It was all too awful to be true, a nightmare from which presently she would wake up.

The rain when it began was so violent that each drop had the impact of a small stone against her unprotected face and head. With a sound of ripping and tearing the superstructure of the little wheelhouse began to come apart. Lying helplessly on the deck, stunned and battered by the storm, Lena waited for the entire boat to disintegrate.

Time ceased to have any meaning. She couldn't say how long it was before the sudden jolt came. In her half stunned way she realised they had struck solid land. The island! Stupefied, she crawled on her hands and knees down the slanting deck and scrambled on to the swamp of mud and stones which was the island's foreshore. She had long since lost her sandals. Shallow water washed over her bare feet as she pulled herself up and tried to get her bearings. There was just enough light left for her to see the towering rock ahead of her. If she could reach it she could climb up on it until she found some crevice into which she could creep for shelter; from the rising river as well as the fury of the storm. Already the water through which she began to wade was half way up to her knees. She pressed on, oblivious to the fate of the boat she had left. There was nothing in her mind now but the sheer animal instinct for survival.

Vaguely she was aware that the launch was breaking up where it lay, the rush of water tearing it apart like giant hands. But she couldn't care . . . couldn't make herself realise it was actually happening. If only the raging of the wind would leave her alone for a moment she might be able to collect her senses.

Desperately she forced herself to assess the situation. At least she was on the island, with a great solid rock to cling to—if only she could reach it. She was wading through long wet grass now and with a shudder thought of . . . *snakes*! If only she could reach the rock! she thought again. She *must* reach it. Help would come to her sooner or later. Rod would be out looking for her. Thank goodness she had left that note on the kitchen table.

Wearing only a thin cotton dress, soaked to the skin, she was shivering violently. But in her efforts to escape from the rising water she was hardly aware of her condition. Stumbling through the clinging grass and whirling water, she found herself at last close to the rock. Her frantic glance searched in the gloom for a foothold so that she could climb up it to safety, though footholds were scarce in the almost smooth surface. Clinging with her fingertips to a narrow outcrop, she dragged herself out of the water.

It was so dark by now that she could no longer see what she was doing. Her bare feet at last found a sizeable crevice and with a final effort she hauled herself to comparative safety. At least she was up out of the water. All she had to do now was to stay where she was, half sitting, half clinging, until help came. How in this darkness would Rod find her? For she was certain he must already be looking for her, and lifting her voice called his name. The sound was drowned by the banshee wailings of the wind. She hadn't known wind could make such a variety of weird noises as it tore through the branches of the trees—vicious, triumphant, a cyclone destroying all that lay in its path. It battered at her as she clung to her refuge, its very force helping to keep her on her narrow ledge, pressed against the bulk of the rock.

There were moments when the sound of the wind was like a human voice wailing its despair. The ghost of the drowned Caloola, Lena thought with a shudder. Was it true that she haunted the island? It was all so eerie that any horror was possible. Tears streamed down Lena's face, mingling with the savage raindrops, but she hardly knew she was weeping. She only knew she was terrified, alone and in mortal peril. If Rod did not come soon it would be too late.

How long she stayed there clinging to the massive volcanic rock she did not know. When the distant flash of light appeared moving about among the trees, on what must have been the river's submerged edge, she thought it was lightning. All it wanted now was a raging thunderstorm and a few thunderbolts falling around her to complete the havoc.

But the light was small and steady, moving through the darkness. Lena gazed at it wide-eyed, afraid to hope—almost beyond the power to think of hope. Dazed, stupefied she watched the light draw nearer. Could it be Rod? she wondered dully, half conscious in her exhaustion. When she opened her mouth to call his name no sound came.

Then she heard his voice. 'Lena!' he cried. 'Lena! Where are you?'

CHAPTER X

'Rod!' The name came out in a shrill scream. Half falling, half scrambling, Lena edged herself off the rock and began wading through the knee-deep water towards the light. Tree branches whipped her face, tossed in the screaming wind; her bare feet were scratched and bleeding. But she scarcely felt their pain in her ecstasy of relief.

Then she saw him, a torch held aloft illuminating him. Wet and bedraggled as herself, he pushed his way through the water towards her. His face seemed all bones and hollows, his eyes dark and wide.

'Lena!' She was in his arms. He was holding her against his breast, tightly, suffocatingly, as if he would never let her go. She could feel his heart pounding beneath his thin rain-soaked shirt.

'Lena!' he breathed her name again—softly this time, close to her ear. 'Oh, Lena, I thought you were lost. God knows what I thought when I saw the launch smashed and piled up against the foreshore of the island. And you were nowhere near it.' He was stroking her dripping hair back from her brow.

She dared not speak or move. It was enough that he was here, that he had come to her rescue. The relief was so great that it robbed her of coherent thought. She only knew Rod was holding her, soothing her; the gentle touch of his hand on her brow filled her with a mindless content. She felt his tenderness engulf her. At that moment the storm and its horrors might never have been.

But too soon the illusion was shattered. The raging of the wind intruded, increasing in force; its banshee wailing screaming in their ears. Once more it was horror and danger which dominated the scene. Somewhere in their vicinity a tree crashed with a tearing sound.

'Let's get out of here!' Rod's voice was rough in its urgency, and he released her from his arms so abruptly that she almost fell over into the rising water. He flashed a torch in her face, scrutinising her anxiously. 'Do you think you can make it back to what's left of the bank? I've got my boat tied up to a tree there.'

'Your small rowing boat?' she asked incredulously —surely too fragile a craft in which to face the savage elements.

'How do you think I got here without the launch? Do you imagine I swam?' His tone was exasperated, impatient, and his hold on her arm was so tight as he urged her along that it was painful. His brief mood of tenderness had vanished. He had been relieved at finding her—that was all. What else could it have been? No doubt he was bitterly angry with her. She had ruined his launch by her irresponsible behaviour.

They had by this time reached the place where it had broken up, and bits of it could be seen in the light of the torch. floating on the water. At the sight of it a sob caught her breath.

'I'm sorry, Rod,' she brought out shakenly. 'Your lovely launch!'

'A pretty complete write-off.' His voice was toneless as he looked at the waterlogged hull, rapidly sinking into the dark swirling torrent.

If only she had not gone rushing off into Latonga this afternoon with no regard for the warnings he had uttered at breakfast time about the danger of the currents in the swollen river! Now it was in full flood.

He was flashing the torch around looking for the row boat. There it was, bobbing about precariously on the end of its straining painter. It looked about as substantial as an eggshell in this raging river! But he was guiding her towards it, helping her into it. Untying the painter, he jumped into the little craft, shouting to Lena in the stern seat to pick up the steering ropes and do what she could with them. He himself was forcing the oars on to the rowlocks, making an effort to head the boat for home.

'Do what you can to keep us on course,' he called above the shrieking of the wind. He had fixed the large torch in the prow so that it cast a pale beam of light ahead of them. He rowed with short, swift strokes, meeting the buffetings of the waves. Perhaps it was the very fragility of the little boat which kept them afloat. Light as a fallen leaf, it skimmed the water.

Then as suddenly as it had come the wind dropped. But in the comparative calm which followed the rain increased, falling in curtains of water about them. The force of the currents too remained to make their progress difficult. Tugging at the steering ropes, Lena did her best to keep the little boat steady, her task made no easier by the water within the boat rising about her ankles.

'Bale out!' Rod urged her. 'Keep on baling.' She had already found the tin for the purpose beneath the stern seat.

She could hear Rod's deep breaths as he pulled at the oars. In the gloom he was no more than a shadowy outline hunched on the central seat. The rowlocks creaked under the straining oars.

His head bowed beneath the onslaught of the rain, Rod suddenly gave a sardonic laugh. It was so unexpected that it startled her.

173

'You *would* get yourself stranded on the island of the ill-fated Caloola, wouldn't you? But the cast for your little drama was all wrong. It ought to have been Pete Foster turning up to drown with you, not me.'

'Nobody's going to drown with me,' Lena cried, goaded to an anger she would not have thought possible in this crisis. How could there be room for anger? But Rod had the power to madden her.

'This is no time for cheap taunts,' she told him. 'If you're annoyed with me for taking the launch out this afternoon just say so and be done with it. I know I was in the wrong. Am I ever in anything else where you're concerned?' Tears threatened. She gulped them down.

'Okay, okay!' Rod's tone was weary. 'Let's leave the bickering for the moment and be thankful we're nearly at Windara.

'Look out with the steering!' he shouted then as an uprooted tree trunk bore down on them. Lena guided them clear of the obstacle with an effort which claimed her whole attention, easing her resentment against Rod. And he had said they were nearly at this nightmare journey's end. Her hands were bleeding now, skinned by the abrasive ropes which had cut into them, straining against the forceful currents. How she had kept the boat more or less on course she would never know. But of course Rod had helped too with his rowing, instinctively feeling the pressure it was necessary to put on each oar in turn.

They did not speak again during the gruelling quarter of an hour which followed. At last in the weak beam of the torch they made out the half submerged landing stage of the Windara property. A few moments later Rod was tying the boat up and helping the exhausted Lena out of it. They had to wade through

174

deep water to find the familiar lane. The little railway line was already awash, and still the rain sluiced down. Doggedly they pressed on in the darkness, Rod holding Lena's arm to keep her from slipping in the mud. When they began to climb the hill which led to the house the flood water was left behind.

'But it won't be for long,' Rod prophesied. 'The cottage will be partly under water before morning. As soon as I've got you indoors I'll have to go down there and salvage what I can of mine and Mandy's belongings.'

'You mean it's going to get worse, this flooding?' Lena asked.

'God alone knows what's going to happen.' Rod's voice was grim. 'I've only seen it as bad as this once before, and then it happened without the aid of a cyclone and a specially high oceanic tide, which is what we've had this afternoon. There were radio warnings about it just before I set out to find you. Serious flooding in Brisbane and all along the coast, helped on by winds of cyclonic force.'

He turned to her angrily. 'What on earth made you take the launch into Latonga this afternoon, when you knew I'd refused to let you use it this morning because of the dangerous currents?'

'I thought they would have subsided,' Lena offered without much conviction.

Rod made an impatient sound. 'And having been lucky enough to get there why did you hang around so long, risking the coming of the storm, and nightfall? Swanning about with Pete Foster, I suppose. He shouldn't have let you set out for home. . . .'

'Don't, Rod!' she interrupted with a gulp that this time refused to be swallowed discreetly. 'I wasn't with Pete.' Her wounded feet were hurting so much that

175

she felt she could hardly take another step. But somehow she must keep going. . . .

'I went into town this afternoon, if you must know, to post an important letter to Mr McKindry, telling him I wanted to return home to England as soon as it could be managed. I asked him if I should refund this month's money, since if I leave I shan't be entitled to it.'

'And it was all so urgent that you couldn't wait to get your letter into the post. Well, I'm afraid there'll be some delay in its delivery now—if indeed it ever reaches its destination. Postal services are sure to suffer if we have a full-scale flood. So it looks as if you'll have to put up with Windara for a little while yet—to say nothing of my distasteful company. Indeed, you'll probably be seeing more of me than usual since I shall have to abandon the cottage in this weather and sleep up at the house.'

She let the sneering allusions pass, too exhausted to answer them. Her limping by this time was obvious, her progress slower and slower.

Becoming aware of her distress, Rod turned the torch on her.

'Good heavens, your feet!' he exclaimed. 'How did you cut them, what's become of your shoes?'

'I lost them in the water right at the start of the storm,' Lena told him. 'I had to walk barefoot across the island to the rock. I must have cut my feet climbing it, looking for a ledge I could crouch on above the rising water.' The words came out mechanically, trailing away indistinctly. She felt her senses grow dim. Was she going to collapse? She held out a hand to Rod to steady herself.

'Here, hold the torch.' He thrust it into her hand. 'You're all in. I'll have to carry you the rest of the

176

way.'

She wanted to protest, but the words wouldn't come. There was strength in his arms as he lifted her up, strength in his straining breaths as he toiled the last few yards up the hill.

Somehow they were indoors at last, blessedly out of the rain, being greeted by Mrs Clarens and a wide-eyed Mandy.

'Get her to bed, she's all in,' Rod gasped, as he dropped Lena rather roughly into the nearest chair. But the journey uphill had not been easy for him. She was no featherweight, Lena thought in helpless misery. Slim as she appeared, there was a shapeliness about her which was far from skinniness.

'I'm all right,' she managed, getting to her feet somewhat unsteadily to prove it. 'I'll be fine when I've had a bath and a rest.' She made her way to the stairs and pulled herself up by the banisters, Mrs Clarens, all concern, following her.

If only she could get to her room without collapsing! Lena thought, aware that Rod was standing below in the hall watching her progress—with an eye, she felt, which would be more impatient than sympathetic.

Tactfully, Mrs Clarens asked no awkward questions as she helped Lena to undress and get into the warm bath. She found adhesive plaster for the scratched feet and hands.

Getting into bed was, at that moment, the nearest approach to heaven Lena could imagine. Mrs Clarens brought her a cup of hot milk laced with rum, but before she had time to drink it she had dropped off into a blessed sleep. She lay sunk in its depths while the night of storm and flood went its tragic way until dawn broke on a watery world.

For three dark, strange days the rain fell and the flood waters rose. Here on the top of the hill the inhabitants of Windara were safe enough, but it was frightening to look out at the expanse of water just beyond and below the garden boundary. Tree tops looked like green bushes just emerging from the deep water and all the lower growth was completely submerged. Before things got too bad Rod had managed to rescue the small rowing boat and tie it up to the garden gate just below the steep path which led to the house. For some time it would be his only means of transport. The ponies too had been led to saftey and were now tethered safely in the paddock at the top of the hill on which the house stood.

Indoors, life went its muted way. There was no gas or electricity. The telephone could no longer function. But Mrs Clarens coped with the domestic details as well as she could, boiling kettles and cooking sketchy meals on a precious oil stove which had been brought out of retirement in the garage and pressed into service. Fortunately there was a supply of oil to feed it.

Mandy, subdued and awestruck by the dimly sensed dangers surrounding them, played with her kitten and her dolls, while Lena limped about doing what she could to amuse the little girl and help Mrs Clarens. But there was hardly enough to occupy her and the days with their ominous import dragged. Only a small transistor linked them with the outside world, bringing news of the horrors which had struck the state. Brisbane had been badly hit, with deep water in the main streets, hundreds of families rendered homeless, their houses destroyed.

As to the cultivated land at Windara, it had, Rod reported grimly, been turned into a watery wilderness, not a sugar cane or a pineapple plant left. Touring the place in the small boat, he had made sure that all his workers had got safely away before things reached their worst. Most of them lived in or near Latonga, where, it was reported the floods were not so bad as elsewhere. Wisely, the little town had been built on rising ground with plenty of drainage available, for although catastrophes of the present dimension were rare the normal seasonal rainfall in that part of Queensland was heavy, and indeed welcome, bringing relief from the summer heat and making the land fruitful.

On the day that the rain ceased and the sun came out the occupants of Windara House gazed at one another in disbelief. It was midday. Rod had just returned from one of his heartbreaking tours of the property and his mood was sombre. Looking at him across the kitchen-dinette table where they were having their midday snack lunch, Lena was shocked by his appearance. There was a stubble of golden beard on his chin and his eyes were hollow. He looked like someone who has suffered a mortal blow and he ate hardly any of the food Mrs Clarens put before him. She, too, was eyeing him with concern.

'Please God the worst is over,' she said with forced cheerfulness, as she got up from the table to draw one of the venetian blinds against the increasing heat of the noonday sun. She turned back to Rod. 'You'll be able to dry out all that stuff now which you brought up from the cottage and the office.'

It was heaped on the verandah outside the kitchen; garments and bedclothes from the cottage, piles of water-sodden papers and documents from the office.

'I can see to it,' Lena offered quickly, pleased at the prospect of having something useful to do. It would help to keep her thoughts from their dreary treadmill, her longing to be free from the horror of the flood, countered by her dread of the moment when she would have to get aboard that plane and head for England, leaving Windara . . . and Rod behind . . . for ever.

She watched him now as his tragic glance withdrew from the nothingness into which he had been staring. There was purpose, even a glimmer of hope in the look he directed at her.

'Perhaps you could start sorting out the office stuff,' he suggested. 'There are wage sheets there somewhere and a bunch of accounts to be sent to the retailers who have been buying our fruit during the past months. There is also,' he added on a note of bitterness, 'a sheaf of bills waiting to be paid. I'd be glad if you'd make a total of them . . . though the lord knows how I'm going to meet them.'

'But surely there's money available?' Lena said.

A question Rod partly evaded. He said, 'The funds I use for paying bills come from the cash I get in from week-to-week sales. Do you imagine any of the retailers are going to be in a position now to meet their obligations; with their shops in ruins, their stock destroyed? Over twenty feet of water in many parts of Brisbane where most of our trade comes from. Don't you realise what that means?' His tone was impatient.

'I thought there was plenty of money in the estate,' Lena said.

'Most of the wealth is in land and crops,' Rod answered obliquely, and without waiting for any further comment from her he strode out of the house.

'He's off in the boat again,' Mrs Clarens deplored, looking after him out of the kitchen window. 'Breaking his heart, touring the damaged areas. There isn't much left of Windara now, I'm afraid. I don't know what the New Zealand beneficiary will think of it, I'm sure.'

Not much left of Windara. Puzzling over just what Mrs Clarens might mean, Lena went out on to the verandah and started sorting the hopeless piles of office stuff, while the older woman rescued clothes and blankets to be hung on the garden clothes lines.

Lena worked on the water-soaked papers all afternoon, spreading them out on the verandah floor boards to dry. Many of them were past saving, but there were others she could just manage to salvage by making fresh copies of them. One of the things Rod had rescued from the office that first day of the floods was the typewriter.

The next day Lena made a temporary office out of the small morning room off the lounge. Finding her installed there busy at her task, Rod was grateful. But all too soon she had used up the small amount of dry paper available . . . a couple of quires Rod had picked up at random the day he was bringing the typewriter.

'I'm stuck now,' she told him, 'until I can get into Brisbane and buy a further supply of paper.'

Rod gave a wry laugh. 'I doubt if you'll find any dry paper for sale in Brisbane for quite a while. You could find some in Latonga, perhaps, but the road and river are still impassable, I'm afraid.'

Two days later the floods were noticeably abating. It was amazing how quickly the water was draining away now that the rain had ceased. And the hours of hot sunshine helped. In little more than a week some semblance of normality was being restored to the stricken state. People were able to leave the refuges to which they had been taken by Army transport, and return to what was left of their homes. The stories of wholesale destruction of property which came through on the transistor were harrowing. Many of the houses had been completely destroyed. Those that remained standing were knee-deep in brown mud and slush. Furniture had been smashed by the force of the water. In some cases every personal and domestic possession had been lost.

In spite of all this and sooner than could have been expected light and power were restored. Mrs Clarens could use the kitchen cooker again. There was hot water for baths and showers. Most heartening of all, the postman arrived one morning bringing a batch of mail. He was met on the verandah by Rod. There was a letter for Lena from Mr McKindry. Recognising the familiar envelope, Rod handed it to her. 'Here's what you've been waiting for. I hope it's good news.'

Lena hurried up to her room to open it in private, half dreading its contents. Absorbed in the tasks of clearing up after the floods, she had pushed her own personal affairs to the back of her mind, relieved indeed to be rid of them. She had almost forgotten the prospect of her return to England. Now, with painful intensity, she read what Mr. McKindry had to say. The letter had been written just before the flood water reached the part of the city in which his office was situated. But he realised the seriousness of the situation.

'I have no idea when this will reach you,' he wrote, 'but when it does, be assured that you are free to leave Windara without any kind of financial obligation. I am sorry that you find yourself unable to fulfil the conditions of your late uncle's will, and that you and Mr Carron have not decided to marry, thereby inheriting the Shannon estate. But provisions were made for just this eventuality in the will. In the event of you and Mr Carron failing to work out the trial period of six months he had suggested it was Mr Shannon's wish that you should both be paid the entire sum made

182

available for the six months indicated. This was not to be revealed to you unless the occasion arose. Now that it has arisen perhaps you will both be good enough to get in touch with me as soon as the present crisis is past; I will then hand over the balance of the money due to you.'

Instead of feeling grateful for her uncle's generosity Lena experienced a sense of shock that she should be free to leave Windara so easily.

It was not until later in the day that Rod, returning from one of his fruitless tours of the derelict lands, asked her what Mr McKindry had had to say. He had found her in the morning room, making out the bills which he had said would not now be paid. But still she perservered with the work. Like Rod and his wanderings over the ruined fields she found distraction in the useless task.

'It seems,' she told him, 'that I'm free to go at any moment, and the whole of the six months' probationary money is to be paid to me.' She handed him the letter.

He made no attempt to read it, his eyes fixed on her with desperate intensity. 'So you can take off as soon as you are able to book a flight,' he said. 'There's nothing to stop you going at once. The airports opened again today . . .'

Lena winced away from the implication. It still seemed quite unreal that in a matter of days she would be thirteen thousand miles . . . a world . . . away from Windara.

'Read what Mr McKindry says,' she urged, indicating the letter he held in his hand. 'There's good news in it for you.'

Dully he obeyed her, his expression unchanging as he scanned the typed pages. 'So you think this is good news,' was his comment when he had finished reading.

'Off you go scot free with a nice bonus. And I'm to do the same. How beautifully simple it all is, isn't it?' His laughter was bitter.

'Not that there's anything to keep me here now,' he added, handing the letter back to her. 'Like to come for a walk round the property and see what the floods have done to it?'

She went with him out into the westering sunlight. Soon it would be sunset time, but for a brief interlude the landscape lay bathed in the kindly glow of early evening. So that the fields through which they walked, although ankle deep in drying mud, still retained a sad beauty. They walked in silence to the top of the hill which formed the apex of the property and saw the acres of pineapple and sugar-cane uprooted by the savagery of the cyclone. Down below on the flats by the river the strawberry fields were a swamp, still partly under water and completely denuded, the entire crop of fruit and plants having been washed into the swiftly flowing river—still a good foot above its normal level.

They stood in silence looking down at the quagmire where once the rosy fruit had grown and ripened.

'A fine inheritance for the New Zealand bloke, isn't it?' Rod brought out presently, his voice sharp with bitterness. 'I don't suppose he would be able to sell it, or even give it away in the condition it's in.'

'But surely it could be put to rights again,' said Lena, unable to bear the hopelessness of Rod's words.

'Only by months of devoted hard work . . . with very little immediate financial return. That's the snag with this kind of property. The wealth is in the soil, not in the bank. It would take some time to build it all up again into the kind of returns on which Tom Shannon's fortunes rested.'

Lena pondered this complicated pronouncement for

a moment. Then she said, 'Perhaps in the circumstances the New Zealander will refuse to have it. If he does,' she added breathlessly, 'you could stay on. Put it all right . . . make the fields and plantations the way they were before the storm. It's *your* land, Rod. You made it the wonderful profitable place it once was. You can't leave it like this.'

He turned to her impatiently. 'What do you care about it? A worthless, watery wilderness.'

'I care about what it means to you,' she answered, her voice not quite steady.

He gave her a startled, enquiring glance. Then he turned away with a shrug. 'Thanks for the sympathy. But it can't really matter all that much to you, can it? You'll be off to England in a day or two, leaving it all behind like a bad dream.'

'A lost dream,' she whispered, and in the silence which followed heard herself say, 'If only it could have turned out the way Uncle Tom wanted it to!'

The sun was a huge burning globe now, sinking beneath the horizon, flooding the whole scene with crimson glory. The incredible Queensland sunset, filling the world with its throbbing rose-red glow.

'It's so beautiful,' Lena said. 'A magic land, even battered and wounded the way it is. You can feel the unconquerable life in it . . .'

Something like hope flashed for an instant in Rod's quick glance. 'It *is* unconquerable,' he asserted. 'These periods of disaster come and go and in their wake the land survives undefeated. If I had even a year in which to tackle the devastation . . .' He left the sentence unfinished with a sigh.

'In all the time I've been here,' he went on then, 'we have never had anything as bad as this cyclone, and it may be years before another one hits us. If it ever

185

does.'

'Don't leave Windara, Rod,' Lena urged. 'Stay with it!'

'If only I could!' His eyes, all dark centres, searched her face desperately.

'A property that is worthless,' she said. 'Or that will be until an incalculable amount of hard work is put into it. Nobody could think you were taking it on for mercenary reasons. And if I stayed with you . . .' her voice faded to a thread of sound, 'that couldn't be for mercenary reasons either.'

'Stayed with me?' he echoed incredulously.

'I know it wouldn't be easy,' she said. 'There wouldn't be much money and lots of hard work. But if only I could feel I was helping you it would be so wonderful.'

Where she got the courage to say all this she didn't know. Only that it had to be said. Rod gazing heart-brokenly at his ruined fields was too much for her, lifting her above all thoughts of selfish timidity.

'Is this the marriage of convenience again?' His tone was brusque and hurtful.

'No, Rod. Oh, Rod, you're making it so hard for me!'

'You're not by any chance trying to tell me that you've obliged Uncle Tom and fallen in love with me?'

The mockery in his tone robbed Lena of her last defences. She covered her eyes with her hands, shutting out the evening glory, the ruined lands, the man at her side. He did not speak or move, leaving her there in her humiliation. When she looked up at last her face was white and drawn.

'It's all right Rod. Forget it. I shouldn't have said anything. I just thought that if one person in a marriage was in love it wouldn't be so bad. I know you

186

can't feel about me the way I feel about you. But if one of us were fulfilling the conditions of Uncle Tom's will . . .'

'Lena!' he cut her short. He stood amid the ruins of the fields looking down at her in growing wonder. 'Lena!' he breathed her name again. 'What a fool I've been all these weeks, suspecting you, belittling you, mistrusting you—only remembering the scornful things you said to me the day we first met.'

'You said scornful things too,' Lena reminded him. 'We got off to a bad start.'

'I'll say we did! And even then I was too aware for comfort of the way I could really feel about you. You were so gallant, so brave—coming out to Windara to help the poor widower! If only you knew how appealing you were!'

She was in his arms then. For a moment he looked down at her uplifted face, then his mouth was hard and hungry on her own. 'Lena . . . oh, darling! I can't believe this is really happening to us. The time I've wasted. It's taken a king-size cyclone to blow my stupidity away.'

They stood gazing at one another, lost in the wonder of their newly discovered love. For Lena it was as if her whole being had melted into the golden evening light. It was all so incredible. She couldn't yet quite take it in. Rod loved her. When she had spoken to him just now it was a lifeline thrown out to him in his despair over the ruined land. A chance to reclaim Windara. It was Windara she had been offering him. But it was so much more than Windara he wanted! The knowledge opened up for her a whole amazing new world. She stood on its threshold, a timorous stranger.

He touched her cheek with a gentle fingertip, tracing the lines of its delicate bone structure, his eyes adoring

187

her.

'It's like being born again,' he said. 'Like the dawn, the sunrise . . . the beginning of a wonderful new day.'

Would it be a day that healed the last of his grieving for Dolores? But that was a question Lena, wisely, did not ask.

They walked down the hill hand in hand. The sun had gone with its customary suddenness and the tropical darkness was falling rapidly. In the house awaiting them the homely lamplight shone.

Seeing it, Rod said, 'It's not a watery wilderness after all that you'll share with me. There's still the house, safe on its hillside. And the land immediately surrounding it was not greatly harmed by the storm . . . the grass and the flowers are left to us.'

'And my jacaranda tree . . .' Lena added. 'Now I'll be able to see it bloom again in the spring. So many springs', she said softly. 'They're all waiting for us. Oh, Rod, I can't believe it's true. But it is!'

They had to stop to kiss again at that. Then Lena was saying, 'You can turn down that job in Sydney now. Mandy won't be uprooted, disturbed . . .'

'She'll have *you*,' Rod said. She's grown to love you, depend on you. I was dreading what a separation from you might do to her.'

'Dear Mandy,' Lena sighed happily. 'And there's Mrs Clarens,' she added more prosaically. 'Perhaps she won't have to go away either.'

'If she could accept the fact that it would be you at the helm now,' Rod qualified it. 'She might prefer to leave. But at least we can offer her a home if she wants it. Lower wages, I'm afraid, but less work. A refuge in her declining years.'

There would be so much to do at Windara house. For a moment Lena's thoughts seethed at the prospect.

All those shabby but pleasant rooms to refurbish gradually. A home. A real home! Not only for Mrs Clarens. There was that sewing machine in the attic, she remembered. She could run up new curtains . . . Her eyes were stars in her uplifted face.

'You look so beautiful, darling. What are you thinking about?' Rod asked.

'Curtains,' she answered, and they both laughed. 'I'm going to make new curtains for all the windows.'

'And I'll redecorate my old bedroom,' Rod said. 'The one in which you and Mandy are now sleeping. Mandy can have the little dressing room next to Mrs Clarens' room. While you and I . . .' He couldn't go on for a moment. Taking her in his arms, he held her close, his lips buried in her hair. 'There's nothing to stop us getting married right away . . . had that thought occurred to you, darling?'

Lena drew a quick breath. 'We'll have to tell Mr McKindry.'

But they weren't really thinking about Mr McKindry as their lips met in a kiss which tried to say everything for which they could find no words.

In the warm darkness they clung to one another, the bright stars above them blossoming in the vast mysterious sky.

Each month from Harlequin

8 NEW FULL LENGTH ROMANCE NOVELS

Listed below are the last three months' releases:

1881	THE END OF THE RAINBOW, Betty Neels
1882	RIDE OUT THE STORM, Jane Donnelley
1883	AUTUMN CONCERTO, Rebecca Stratton
1884	THE GOLD OF NOON, Essie Summers
1885	PROUD CITADEL, Elizabeth Hoy
1886	TAKE ALL MY LOVES, Janice Gray
1887	LOVE AND LUCY BROWN, Joyce Dingwell
1888	THE BONDS OF MATRIMONY, Elizabeth Hunter
1889	REEDS OF HONEY, Margaret Way
1890	TELL ME MY FORTUNE, Mary Burchell
1891	SCORCHED WINGS, Elizabeth Ashton
1892	THE HOUSE CALLED SAKURA, Katrina Britt
1893	IF DREAMS CAME TRUE, Rozella Lake
1894	QUICKSILVER SUMMER, Dorothy Cork
1895	GLEN OF SIGHS, Lucy Gillen
1896	THE WIDE FIELDS OF HOME, Jane Arbor
1897	WESTHAMPTON ROYAL, Sheila Douglas
1898	FIREBIRD, Rebecca Stratton
1899	WINDS FROM THE SEA, Margaret Pargeter
1900	MOONRISE OVER THE MOUNTAINS, Lilian Peake
1901	THE BLUE JACARANDA, Elizabeth Hoy
1902	THE MAN AT THE HELM, Henrietta Reid
1903	COUNTRY OF THE VINE, Mary Wibberley
1904	THE CORNISH HEARTH, Isobel Chace

These titles are available at your local bookseller, or through the Harlequin Reader Service, M.P.O. Box 707, Niagara Falls, N.Y. 14302; Canadian address 649 Ontario St., Stratford, Ont. N5A 6W4.

Have You Missed Any of These

Harlequin Romances?

Have You Missed Any of These Harlequin Romances?